ALSO BY
MICHAEL THOMAS PERONE

The Darkest Side:
A Collection of Twisted Nursery Rhymes

Lists, Life, and Other Unimportant Details:
Musings by Michael Thomas Perone

To Elspeth,
Enjoy the ride!

DANGER PEAK

PEAK

A KID ADVENTURE

MICHAEL THOMAS PERONE

Danger Peak

Published by Wheatmark®
2030 East Speedway Boulevard, Suite 106
Tucson, Arizona 85719 USA
www.wheatmark.com

ISBN: 978-1-62787-950-7 (paperback)
ISBN: 978-1-62787-951-4 (ebook)
LCCN: 2022903105

Bulk ordering discounts are available through Wheatmark, Inc.
For more information, email orders@wheatmark.com or call
1-888-934-0888.

for Steven

CONTENTS

PROLOGUE

October 1989

Thirteen-year-old Robert Kin joyfully, almost mischievously, weaved his green customizable motorbike through the generic, manufactured labyrinth of his suburban town's roads. Zipping along the treelined streets, he felt like a flying squirrel leaping from branch to branch. He liked to imagine the bony tree fingers were reaching out to him as he tried to outrace their grasp, and with the visor open on his safety helmet, he could feel the wind whipping at his face like a plunging skydiver.

Robert leaned gracefully into the turns until his body was almost parallel with the pavement. It was as if the bike were a part of him. As he scanned the rapidly approaching streets, the comforting vibration of the engine, quick burst of acceleration from the twist of the throttle, and jolt of noise made him feel like a god surveying his world. For Robert, the possibility of losing control, yet maintaining full control at all times, was the purest form of freedom. This level of exhilaration inspired him to create his town's local dirt-bike club, the Wild Boars, with his best friend, Chris, and their short, often put-upon sidekick, Rinnie.

As he rode down the street, Robert noted the beauty of the leaves changing color and cursed the days growing shorter, which meant less time to ride his beloved bike. Fall was a particularly poignant season.

Robert purposefully rolled his vehicle through the fall foliage lining the cracked pavement. As he plowed through small piles of auburn-painted leaves just to hear the satisfying crunch, he dryly noted to himself, "Nature's garbage." This autumnal path of crispy detritus led him to his favorite landmark, the place he turned to time and again to get away from his small town and the even smaller-minded people within it.

Feeling somewhat like a soldier on a mission, he turned one last corner to enter the small patch of forest just outside the city limits. Slowing his bike to a stop, he switched the motor off and then dismounted. After removing his helmet, Robert sauntered up to the rusty gate emblazoned with the landmark's name. The chill fall wind whipped his sandy-brown hair, blocking his chestnut eyes. Annoyed, the seventh grader brushed his locks aside to read the dingy sign that seemed to have stood since time immemorial: "DANGER PEAK."

There it was. It loomed overhead like a natural skyscraper, his town blanketed in its direct shadow. In order to see the entire mountain, Robert had to crane his head back at an unnatural angle. It smarted something awful, but the view was worth it. Danger Peak was almost twelve thousand feet high—just over two miles—and no one, not him or any of his friends— had been able to reach the top. Its peak was called insurmountable not just because of its height. Legends sprung from those brave enough to attempt the climb of an eerie mist that clung near the peak and obscured their view; gargantuan, fast-moving boulders that seemed to fling themselves at climbers from out of the ether; and, as if that weren't enough, mysterious weather that welcomed travelers with spontaneous thunderstorms and gale-force winds. No matter what time of year it was or how beautiful the climate below, you could be certain all hell was breaking loose at the top of Danger Peak. It seemed supernatural. All of these obstacles mocked those intrepid explorers, daring them to once and for all conquer their neighborhood's star landmark.

With a series of traps this diabolical, Robert and his friends reasoned there must be something spectacular the mountain was guarding at its peak: a pot of gold perhaps, like the fabled rainbow's end, or maybe even a mystical secret of the universe.

The only glimmer of hope of scaling this impossible peak was the curious path winding its way toward the zenith. Somehow a dirt-bike trail had been carved out of the mountain's side. Some say it was manmade, but Robert always wondered how that could be since no one had made it to the top—at least no one had made it back alive. In a way, the mountain's trail was more a tease than a promise; it only made the journey more frustrating. Even with the aid of a motorbike, you still had to face the daunting gauntlet of mists, boulders, and never-ending storms. You still had to see through impenetrable fog and dodge deadly lightning strikes.

In fact, the closest someone had come to besting the mountain was Robert's older brother, Danny, the year before. The high-school junior made it just over half-way before succumbing to the mount's various traps. With the aid of a helicopter, the authorities found his body near the midpoint—his bike, in pieces, fifty feet away.

But that wouldn't stop Robert. As leader of the Wild Boars, he knew he and his pals had to find a way to top Danger Peak. It was their one shot at becoming legends in the eyes of their school and hometown. More than that, it was his dream. Robert would find a way to be the first to scale the mountain . . . or die trying.

1

THE WILD BOARS

"You went back to Danger Peak . . . *again?*" Chris, Robert's best friend since kindergarten, asked.

Chris, Robert, and their younger friend Rinnie were holding another meeting of their Wild Boars club in the large treehouse in Robert's backyard. Chris and Rinnie's dirt bikes were still parked at the wide, bumpy base of the ancient tree. Chris's blue bike dwarfed Rinnie's considerably; Rinnie's gray bike resembled the first draft of Chris's fully developed model. The younger boy's bike was not only smaller but also less powerful than Chris's or Robert's, and he was often teased that it wasn't much faster than a regular pedal-powered bicycle.

Perched in the yellow-and-orange-streaked sky of the late autumnal afternoon, the clubhouse was their stronghold against the outside adult world. As the wistful chorus of Don Henley's "Boys of Summer" drifted from Robert's miniature AM/FM radio mounted on the tanned '70s wood paneling that made up the majority of their ramshackle treehouse, Robert musingly considered a title change to "Boys of Fall."

"Man, you are *obsessed*!" Chris exclaimed, leaning back against the wall, almost inadvertently switching the radio off.

"Yeah," the short, pudgy Rinnie chimed in as he casually flipped through an issue of *Nintendo Power* magazine, "and you're also preoccupied!"

Chris rolled his eyes. "That means the same thing, dorkus," he taunted their pint-sized sidekick. "How did you graduate grammar school with us again?"

"I copied my tests off your mom," Rinnie wisecracked, tousling his ratty, rust-colored hair triumphantly. With that, Chris went in for a windup with his fist, but Robert, ever the peacemaker between the two, blocked him.

"That's enough, you guys," he said. "I didn't call this meeting to start another fight."

"Then why *did* you call this meeting?" Chris asked, gazing around the circular treehouse. A cartoon wall calendar featuring a black cat sticking its head out of the maws of a rotting jack-o'-lantern signified the month of October, and various magazine photos of specialized motorbikes adorned the walls. Then his eyes fell on Robert's handmade poster that sported a crudely drawn purple boar screeching by on a motorbike while shouting their club's motto in a hovering word balloon: "JUST HAVE FUN!"

"To just have fun?" Chris answered his own question, almost duty-bound.

"No," Robert said immediately. Then, sensing his friends' disappointment, he changed his tone and corrected himself. "Well, yes and no."

"What's *that* supposed to mean?" Rinnie asked. Rinnie was a sweet kid but a little slow. He was—as some impolite company would whisper behind his back—the so-called runt of the litter. With his short stature, hunched-over posture, and dirty hair, he resembled a rat. Occasionally, Chris would remind him of this in no uncertain terms, but this time was different.

"Believe it or not, I have to agree with Rinnie," Chris admitted.

Robert pensively stared into the middle distance. Absently, he mused on how Chris's straight jet-black hair and emerald eyes mirrored those of the calendar's Halloween cat. He would've stood up to pace the room if it were big enough. As it was, even though his club was large by treehouse standards, the three of them had almost outgrown its one room since it had been built eight years before by his dad and brother, Danny. In fact, the treehouse was specifically built atop the tall, proud oak with Danny in mind, and subconsciously, Robert always felt like he was trespassing—especially after his brother's death. It was like standing your army on hallowed ground, planting your flag on someone's grave.

"Well?" Chris asked Robert impatiently, breaking his daydream.

"Oh, sorry," Robert apologized.

"Apology accepted," Rinnie said cheerfully.

"He was talking to me, butt wipe," Chris spat.

"Oh, 'butt wipe,'" Rinnie mocked. "That's a new one. Very classy."

"Remind me," Chris then said, turning to Robert, "why do we let him in here?"

Robert was defiant. "I let him in here because it's *my* treehouse," he said, defending the oft-picked-on Rinnie.

"Thanks, man," Rinnie said.

"No problem." Robert smiled.

Chris screwed his eyes tightly, daring himself to correct his friend. "I thought this was *Danny's* treehouse," he said.

Robert inhaled deeply. "Right," he said.

"Hey," Rinnie interjected and pointed to his magazine, "do you guys know about the Konami cheat code?"

Chris suddenly lunged at Rinnie, rudely ripping his *Nintendo Power* away, and ordered, "Gimme that!"

"Stop," Rinnie protested. "I just got it in the mail this morning!"

"Enough!" Robert shouted. At last, he gave his team the meeting's agenda. "I think we should scale Danger Peak once and for all."

"But *hoooww?*" Rinnie whined. Now even *Robert* was getting annoyed with him.

This time, it was Chris's turn to defend Rinnie. "What I think he means is," he softly began, "it's been tried before. You know, Danny . . ." He purposefully let his words trail off. He felt he had already been pushing it with his former insensitive comment about the treehouse rightfully belonging to Robert's brother. From the corner of his eye, the calendar cat seemed to be mocking him.

"I know," Robert replied, "and that's why we have to try it ourselves, for Danny's sake."

"Do you think he *cares?*" Rinnie asked in a surprising outburst. "I mean, he's six feet in the—" Robert shot Rinnie a look that made him catch himself, and Rinnie's cheeks immediately flushed crimson. Chris coiled his fist for another smackdown when they all heard Robert's mother call merrily from outside their clubhouse.

"Robby, come in to eat, and say goodbye to your friends!"

Breaking the ice, Chris was the first to speak. "Your mom still calls you 'Robby'?" he asked. A brief pause, and then the three friends erupted into nervous laughter. Not wanting to end on a fight, Robert put out his right hand, palm down, and announced their other catchphrase: "Friends to the end."

"Friends to the end," Chris and Rinnie repeated, placing their hands on top of his.

2

FAMILY DINNER

"Pass the potatoes, Mom," Robert asked his mother, Donna, at the dinner table. Immediately, Stan, his father, arched his right eyebrow, a telltale sign of disapproval. Robert quickly corrected himself. "*Please*," he added.

"Sure, sweetie," she said warmly, passing the homemade bowl to her beloved son. Earlier that year, in an effort to bury the pain of losing her older son, she had taken a pottery course at night. Despite months of work, she eventually concluded that it didn't do much except add odd-shaped, multicolored dinnerware to the table. The pieces may not have been pretty, but she was committed to using them all the same for the time, effort, and expense she sacrificed.

Stan turned toward his wife. "What's with this 'sweetie' stuff?" he asked with derision as Robert shoveled a heaping glob of mashed potatoes onto his plate—another homemade piece by his mom. "The kid's a teenager now, for Christ's sake."

"No, it's okay," Robert defended his mom as he nervously munched on his mashed potatoes. "I don't mind when we're alone. It's just, you know, in public, like, if you could stop calling me 'Robby' in front of my friends. It's embarrassing."

Donna was about to answer her son when Stan cut her off. "I'll tell you what's embarrassing," he began, turning toward his son. "It's you still hanging out with those losers."

"They're not losers, Dad." Now Robert was faced with defending his friends. For some reason, he always felt like he was on trial when talking to his father.

"They're a stupid gang is what they are," Stan snapped. "Why can't you be more like Danny?" He nearly regretted the question as soon as it left his mouth, not necessarily because he didn't mean it but because it gave his hand away.

Robert turned toward the empty chair at their dinner table. Sadly, his mother still made a setting for her elder son, including one of her ugly handmade dinner plates, as if Danny would one day just miraculously stride through the front door with a bemused grin on his face. As if it were all a big misunderstanding from some corny 1960s sitcom. "Sorry to keep you folks worryin'!" he'd likely say. "I went down to the general store to get bait for the ol' fishin' pole and took the long way home. Boy howdy, did I get *lost*!" Of course, Danny certainly didn't talk that way when he was alive.

"That isn't fair," his mother finally said, breaking the tension in the air and also busting Robert's day-dream bubble with an almost audible pop. His mom usually had his back, but Robert also felt like there were some battles he should learn to fight himself. After all, he couldn't rely on his mother for the rest of his life.

Summoning up an ounce of courage, Robert faced his stern father and said, "I'm *not* Danny, Dad. I'm Robert. And I'm sorry if that disappoints you." With that, he got up from his seat and strode toward the staircase that led to his bedroom.

"Hey, boy," Stan called after his son. "I didn't say you could leave the table!"

Robert kept walking, pretending he couldn't hear him.

"Let him go," his mother said just before they heard the loud bang of Robert's bedroom door slamming shut.

Disgusted and frustrated, Stan wiped his mouth with a napkin and left the table, leaving Donna by her-self to stare at the extra empty chairs.

Stan decided to work in his so-called "man cave," which had been converted from Danny's old bedroom. Replacing everything that Danny owned—his bed, his *Knight Rider* poster, a bookcase featuring reams of manuals on dirt-bike maintenance, a Walkman with a copy of Van Halen's *1984* in the cassette holder—with his own shelves of metallic knickknacks, a large work-bench, and various tools strewn about, it was like he was trying to erase his older son's memory. Stan figured if he could do that, maybe he could also erase the pain.

On the way to his cave, Stan passed Robert's bedroom door, still defiantly locked shut. Pausing hesitantly just outside it, he posed his curled knuckles near the brown balsawood, prepared to rap them against the door. He wasn't sure what to say. A makeshift apology sprung to mind, but thinking better of it, he retreated to his cave to fiddle with his homegrown electronics. After all, he'd never had to admit he was wrong before.

3

FIRST FLASHBACK

Danny's two-wheeled machine was a beautiful master-piece to behold. Its pleasingly sculpted, aerodynamic shell was painted cherry red everywhere save the bold canary lightning bolt flashing across the side. In the nearly dark, overstuffed garage, it looked poised for action, like a toy vehicle come to life. Danny surveyed his "baby" once more, the dirt bike of his dreams, before making the final adjustments. Surrounded by his Led Zeppelin and Who posters on the walls and crouched over the bike, Danny prepared to tighten the lug nuts that fastened the front tire to the bike's frame.

"Hand me the wrench, will ya, Rob?" he asked his younger brother.

"Uh, sure," Robert replied, handing him the closest tool in his reach. Without looking, Danny grabbed it and then, after a confused pause, turned back to his kid brother.

"This is a screwdriver, buddy."

"Oh yeah," the twelve-year-old Robert sputtered. "I knew that. It's just—I wanted you to have it as quickly as possible."

"Remember what I told you," Danny began. "Accuracy, not speed."

"Right," Robert said, nodding solemnly. Danny's small transistor radio sat on a shelf nearby, and Phil Collins was singing about an invisible touch. Robert used to think he was saying "*invincible* touch."

Noticing his brother was losing focus, Danny briskly snapped his fingers in front of his face and instructed, "You need to pay attention to what I'm doing, Robert. You have to learn how to take care of your own bike that Dad bought. I'm not going to be around forever." Another pause as he stared his kid brother down with wise eyes. "Well?" he asked, trying not to lose his patience.

"Oh yeah, right," Robert again stammered and then retrieved the correct tool this time. Danny agreeably grabbed the adjustable wrench, fidgeted with its settings to gauge the right gap, and then went to work.

Suddenly, a commercial blared from the radio, interrupting the Genesis hit: "When you need your floors to look their very best, Comet is better than the rest!"

"Hey, Danny," Robert said, a hint of nostalgia in

his voice. "Remember this?" He began singing a parody of the jingle. "Comet, it makes your mouth turn green!"

Recognizing the memory, Danny smiled and joined in the melody. "Comet, it tastes like gasoline."

"Comet," Robert continued, "makes you vomit."

Now the brothers sang together: "So try some Comet—and vomit—today!" They both laughed like naughty schoolboys. Robert couldn't remember the last time they acted this way, like they were little kids again. It felt wonderful.

It was stiflingly hot in the garage, and Robert noticed Danny needed to repeatedly wipe his forehead with its dripping perspiration. Sensing his need, and before his older brother could cue him, Robert snatched a torn rag by his feet and held it out to Danny. Immersed in his work of attaching the new tire, Danny briefly peered up at the outstretched offering.

"What's that for?" he asked.

"For your forehead," Robert responded. "You're sweating."

"Dude," Danny said, almost laughing, "look a little closer. It's a dirt rag. I already used it earlier to wipe off some oil from the motor." Robert inspected the rag and saw what Danny meant: there was a thick oily smudge streaked right down the center when he opened it. Robert threw the rag down again on the garage floor in disgust. He desperately wanted to make his big brother happy, but it seemed he couldn't do anything right.

"What's the matter, man?" Danny asked, continuing to tighten the bolt before moving on to the back tire.

"Nothin'." It was Robert's usual reply.

"Nothin'," Danny repeated, teasingly using Robert's squeak of a preadolescent voice. "Nothin' doesn't sound like nothing to me."

"It's just," Robert began, "since you got into this hobby a few years ago, you don't have much time for me."

"What're you talking about?" Danny asked. "We still hang out."

"Not as much as before," Robert challenged. "Not since you entered high school."

Danny shuffled his crouch over to the rear tire to make the same adjustments he had made on the front. After a few turns of his wrench, he finally responded, almost quixotically, "High school's a whole new ballgame."

Robert dared himself to answer with the first question that popped into his young, still-forming brain: "What's that supposed to mean?"

Danny's response was immediate. "It means I've got a lot of other things going on now, man," he said, his patience gone. "A lot more tests and quizzes. A lot more homework. I need to start looking at colleges soon. Not to mention girls."

Robert's eyes betrayed him on Danny's last word. He was almost jealous of the number of dates his brother brought home each weekend. At only twelve,

Robert wasn't necessarily interested in going on those dates himself, but he *was* jealous of the amount of time and attention his former playing partner was giving them. Robert missed the days of reenacting scenes from *Star Wars* during their weekly "sleepover" party. They would hide under the blankets of Danny's huge bed, pretending it was the cockpit of the Millennium Falcon. Danny would be Han Solo, and Robert would always be Luke Skywalker. Even though Luke was ostensibly the de facto hero of the film, Robert would want to play Han every once in a while, to no avail. Danny reasoned it was because Han was older than Luke, so their chosen roles made sense, but Robert knew that the real reason was because Han was cooler, and Danny didn't want to surrender his character.

Remembering playing with his brother under the cloak of darkness gave Robert goosebumps. It was like their shared secret. And although it was only a few years ago, it felt like a lifetime.

"What're you thinkin' about, buddy?" Danny asked, breaking another one of Robert's daydreams. "Nothin'?" he again jokily mocked his brother's chosen favorite word. "Your head's always in the clouds," he added in a way that Robert knew Danny wasn't mocking him, just making a matter-of-fact observation. His mention of clouds got Robert thinking of Cloud City and *Star Wars* again, so he revealed what was on his mind and told him of his childhood memory.

"I was just thinking about the sleepovers we used

to have," he said. "You know, playing with old toys and pretending we're Han and Luke."

Danny cocked his head back to laugh, and it set off a little heartache in Robert. Noticing this, Danny pulled himself back. "I remember. We used to pretend to strap on jetpacks and rocket downstairs Saturday mornings to eat cereal and watch cartoons."

"Yeah!" Robert replied like an excited child. His cheeks flushed red as Danny smiled.

"We'll still do those things, Robert."

"Sure we will," Robert answered, unconvinced. "It seems you're interested in *other* sleepovers." Danny looked at Robert, puzzled, until Robert filled in the blanks. "I like Gina," he said. "You've always had a thing for redheads."

Ignoring the mention of his latest conquest, Danny tried to reassure his brother. "You know," he said, "we're still best friends."

Robert looked at his feet, not wanting to make eye contact. "I know."

"Remember what I taught you?" Danny asked.

"Accuracy, not speed?"

"No, the other thing."

"Oh yeah," Robert said, reaching out his right hand, palm down. Danny reciprocated, placing his right palm on top of the back of Robert's hand.

"Friends to the end," they said in unison.

4

THE PLAN

As the Wild Boars sat at their designated table in the school cafeteria, the familiar odor of steamed veggies, stale pizza, and chocolate milk, queasily mixed with the astringent sting of antiseptic cleanser, wafted through the air and made it difficult to finish lunch. At least it did for Robert and Rinnie, but Chris could eat anything. At the moment, he seemed to be trying to stuff as many French fries into his mouth as he could without suffocating. As usual, Robert made a nauseated face, while Rinnie passively flipped through a Batman comic.

"I don't get it," Rinnie said. "The Joker isn't even in this. And who's this Riddler guy? This is nothing like the movie!"

Chris rolled his eyes before downing another greasy French fry. "Rinnie, you *do* realize that you're not reading the comic-book adaptation of the movie that came out this summer and that Batman comics have actually been around for fifty years?"

"Uh, yeah," Rinnie lied, "of course I knew that."

"Of *course*," Chris sarcastically replied with another eye roll for added emphasis.

"I mean," Rinnie continued, his red embarrassed face belying his words, "otherwise, it would've been a waste of my money if I didn't know. Anyway, I wish *I* could be a vigilante," he suddenly said, playing mournfully with his creamed spinach. "They tagged me again. Vinny and his football jerks spray-painted my locker."

"What was it this time?" Chris asked. "'Rinnie the runt'?" Both Chris and Robert laughed.

"No, that was last month," Rinnie explained with downcast eyes. "This time, they went after all of us." Chris and Robert weren't laughing anymore. "They wrote 'Wild BORES' with 'O-R-E-S' instead of 'O-A-R-S.' I have to admit that's pretty clever for a bunch of jocks. I'm surprised they know what a homophone is."

"Those dirt bags!" Chris cursed, throwing a French fry down on his cafeteria tray in disgust. Normally, Chris would eat anything, but he had suddenly lost his appetite.

"Yeah," Robert agreed, "who do they think they are?"

"Um, the most popular guys in school," Rinnie rightfully reported. "And besides," he continued, "you guys didn't seem to care when they were just picking on me."

"You just answered your own question," Chris pointed out a bit cruelly.

Robert nodded. "Taking a shot at all of us was uncalled for," he said. "This is a matter of pride."

"If it's a shot at all of us," Rinnie began, "why am I always the only one who has to clean off his locker?"

Chris patted him on the back for encouragement. "Because you're an easy target, buddy," he said.

"That isn't very comforting," Rinnie replied, attempting to ease the pain with another gulp of chocolate milk like it was a shot of vodka.

Robert began losing patience. There was much that needed to be discussed, and so far, he was failing at reining in his friends' short attention spans. Before Chris could respond to Rinnie, he leaned into the other two to divulge his plans. "Guys, I need to talk to you about something," he began.

Suddenly, Barbara, Rinnie's school crush, walked by their table to empty her lunch in the nearby trashcan and chat with some friends. Rinnie gazed adoringly at her brunette ponytail bobbing past him.

"Hey, babe," Rinnie called.

"My name's Barbara, creep-o!" she replied.

Chris immediately laughed, but Rinnie was undaunted. "You guys laugh, but I'm tellin' ya, I think I'm wearing her down."

Chris rolled his eyes and swallowed another fry glazed with ketchup. "Yeah, you've only been chasing her since, what, the third grade? With dedication like that, I'm sure she'll come around by our high-school graduation."

Robert banged the table with his fist like a judge's gavel. "Will you guys knock it off?" he asked. "There isn't much time left in the period, and I want to get down to business."

"You're always all business, Rob," Chris noted, almost scolding.

"Well, I *am* the leader of this club," Robert countered.

"So what's up?" Chris asked nonchalantly.

"I've been thinking about Danger Peak."

"*There's* a surprise," Rinnie sarcastically spat.

"Shut up, Rinnie," Chris said. "Go on, Robert."

"I know it seems impossible," Robert admitted. "Hell, it's how my brother . . ." His words trailed off as his two friends, preserving his dignity, pretended not to notice. "Well, you know," he continued. "Anyway, no regular motorbike can reach the top, right?"

"Right," Chris agreed.

Robert eyed a picture of Batman's utility belt displayed prominently on an open page of Rinnie's comic book, which gave him an idea. "Then we simply can't use a regular motorbike. We have to build a better one."

"But how?" Rinnie asked.

"It's like Batman's utility belt," Robert explained, pointing at Rinnie's comic on the table in front of them. "To defeat the bad guys, he has to use his inventions."

"Leave Batman out of this!" Rinnie defensively shouted.

Ignoring Rinnie's ridiculous outburst, Chris reasoned, "How are we going to reinvent our dirt bikes, Robert? We're not mechanics."

"No," Robert conceded, "but my brother was, and he taught me almost everything he knew."

"He did?" Chris asked, almost offended that his best friend kept that information from him over the years.

"Well, I watched him fix up his bike a lot anyway."

Now it was Rinnie's turn to speak. "Yeah, but if your brother was so smart, how come he—"

Chris cut him down with his eyes. "Rinnie," he warned. "Don't *even*."

Robert could tell he was failing to rally his troops, so to speak. Just then, he noticed Rinnie playing with the cheese on his hamburger, and that inspired another analogy. "It's like building a better mousetrap," he said.

"But we're not trying to catch mice," Rinnie retorted.

"It's a metaphor, doofus," Chris admonished.

"Actually," Rinnie corrected, "it's a simile since he used the word 'like.'"

"Whatever!" Chris shouted, throwing his hands in the air in frustration. Then, turning to Robert, he added, "I like your plan, man."

"Oh, you're a fan of his plan?" Rinnie teased in rhyme. "Is it grand?" Before Chris could chide him again, Rinnie addressed their leader. "What are you going to call it?"

Robert paused for dramatic emphasis. Then, when he felt his friends were ready, he announced, "The Action Bike." Another pause, and then both Chris and Rinnie burst into incredulous laughter, much to Robert's chagrin.

"Sorry, Rob," Rinnie said between fits of giggles, "but that's pretty lame."

"Yeah," Chris confessed, "I hate to say this, but I have to agree with Rinnie."

"Have any better ideas?" Robert asked, obviously annoyed.

"How about Excitebike?" Rinnie suggested. "That's my favorite Nintendo game." Chris raised his eyebrows, apparently pleased with the new moniker.

"It's already been taken," Robert said dismissively. "Besides, the name's not important. It's what it can do."

"Yeah," Rinnie interjected, suddenly excited. "If it works and we actually reach the top, we can make a lot of mondo cash with the endorsement deals alone!"

Chris rolled his eyes at Rinnie's lingo. "Who says 'mondo' anymore?" he asked no one in particular.

"At least I don't still say 'mint,'" Rinnie retorted.

Just at that moment, Vinny, the school's resident bully, passed by and threw his leftover creamed spinach and fries onto their table, splashing them with ketchup and other undesirables.

"How ya doin', Wild Snores?" he taunted, stalking

off with wide, confident strides. A nearby lunch table filled with jocks laughed in unison. On his way back, Vinny loudly high-fived one of his pals sitting at the end.

After an embarrassed silence, Rinnie shook his head in disgust and sighed. "Man, that was a good one too," he said. "I *knew* we should've named ourselves the Dashing Dinos."

"Shut up, Rinnie," both Robert and Chris said just as Barbara walked back to her table from the garbage bin. Passing by, she briefly eyed the mess on their table and then attempted to stifle a giggle.

Although Robert and Chris were even more mortified, Rinnie, of course, saw this as an opening and turned to his friends. "Ya see?" he asked. "If that's not flirting, I don't know what is."

5

THE TOOLS

First things first, Robert thought. Before he could build the better motorbike, he needed the tools to do so. His brother used to always say, "If you have the tools, you have the talent," but he suspected he stole that line from *Ghostbusters*, one of their favorite movies. Robert didn't have the money for an expensive toolset, and the only one he knew who had the right tools for the job was his father. The only problem was he would never let Robert borrow his precious tools.

Stan was a man who valued two things most of all: his prized tools and his alone time. Lately, he had plenty of the latter now that his so-called "favorite son" had passed, and he had little time for his younger one. Stan would spend hours fixing various gadgets with those tools in his blue-tinted man cave. In a way, they were closer to him than his own family. Robert often wondered about the secrets only those tools knew, and despite how he was treated, he also felt a little sorry for his dad, thinking that playing with his tools in Danny's old bedroom was the only way he knew how to mourn.

Robert wasn't too proud of having to snatch his father's toolbox, but he didn't see any other way around it. If he wanted to make his dream come true and scale that mountain, he was going to have to make some sacrifices, including compromising his own personal morals. Robert knew how important those tools were to his dad, so he needed to find the perfect window of time in which to swipe them.

That opportunity arrived when Stan's favorite quiz gameshow came on at seven o'clock at night. His father would normally break a six-pack open and, though guzzling enough beer throughout the half-hour program to drown a rat, still manage to answer most of the show's questions correctly. Robert often thought his father, armed with a wealth of arcane knowledge and blessed with handyman skills, could've been a genius inventor if he only applied himself, but family life and general laziness had destroyed any ambitions he may have once had in his youth.

As soon as he saw his father plop down on the bed in his room and turn on the TV just a minute before 7 p.m., Robert made his move. He heard the first can of beer pop open and fizz as he crept into his dad's man cave down the hall. The dark-blue room was an inventor's mad design: long steel shelves lined three of the four bare walls, each with multiple drawers filled with assorted electronic parts. To Robert and his mom, they were simply junk, but to his father, they were price- less. He was still trying to build the better mousetrap, which was part of Robert's inspiration earlier that day in the cafeteria.

A long black desk stood guard in front of the last wall, and behind that desk was Stan's secret stash. It's where he kept the toolbox with his most important tools. Stan didn't think anyone else knew the location, but it was an open secret in the family. He would tin- ker in that room so often, usually half drunk or at least a little buzzed, that he would forget to close the door behind him, so Robert and his mom could see exactly where he kept that box.

Not wanting to draw attention to himself, Robert purposefully didn't put the light on in the room. He knew he wasn't supposed to be there, so he wanted to get in and out in as smooth an operation as possi- ble. Robert softly crept to the large desk in the back of the room and angled his long bony arm behind it at a crooked angle to blindly find the handle on top of the toolbox in the dark. After a few false grasps, he man- aged to find it and confidently pull the box out from behind the desk. Robert hadn't realized how heavy it was and almost dropped it as the box cleared the top of the desk, but he managed to bring it under con- trol by hugging it tightly to his chest. All safe. Robert wiped his sweaty brow with the back of his unused hand when, suddenly, he heard from behind, "What're you doing here?"

Robert spun around suspiciously with the toolbox in his hand to lock eyes with his father, who stood under the door's arch and filled the frame. Robert reasoned he must have resembled the robber at the bank with his hand in the cookie jar. He was never good at metaphors.

Robert surmised that his dad was already half drunk and clearly not in the cheeriest of moods. *So much for my window of time*, he thought. He had forgotten about the commercials. Robert stared at the aluminum beer can still clutched in his father's hand as Stan, in turn, stared at his treasured toolbox in his son's hand. After a quarter of a minute, Stan impatiently repeated his question, this time more firmly, as he stepped aggressively into the room. "I asked what the hell you're doing in here, Robert?" Stan tended to swear when he drank.

"I need to borrow your toolbox," Robert meekly answered.

"Then why didn't you just ask me for it?"

Putting on a brave face, Robert said, "'Cause I knew you wouldn't let me."

His father took another long slug from his can, wiped his mouth, and replied, "You're damn right about that. Now put it back."

Desperate, Robert succumbed to bargaining. "But you don't understand, Dad," he began, his nervous voice becoming louder and more panicky with each word as he fumbled with a makeshift explanation.

"I need to fix up my bike and do what Danny never could. I need to scale Danger Peak once and for all!"

His father smarted like he was punched in the face. "Why the hell would you want to do *that*? It's what got Danny killed!"

"I want to do it to make him proud," Robert answered. When he realized that excuse wasn't good enough, he added, "To make *you* proud."

"Well, you're sure off to a great start," his dad sarcastically spat, still glaring at the toolbox in Robert's hand. He shook his head solemnly and then softly said, almost to himself, "Danny would never do this." Robert winced as if his father had just lashed him across the face with his belt. Sensing this, Stan felt a twinge of sympathy. "You're a good kid, Robert. Why are you doing this?"

"Because it's my dream to climb that mountain!" Robert was stammering now, almost like a little child.

Shifting gears, and somewhat recognizing a bit of Robert in himself, Stan softened his approach. "I had dreams once too, kid," he said wistfully while adjusting his blocky glasses. "I wanted to be a fighter pilot for the Air Force, but my vision—or lack of it—kept me out. But I've no regrets. Your mother often reminds me that if I had achieved my dream, I could've been shot down behind enemy lines. Then I wouldn't have gone on to marry her, and you wouldn't have been born."

"Yeah," Robert added, "and Danny wouldn't have been born either . . . only to die seventeen years later."

"Don't talk like that."

"Well, it's true!"

"Be thankful for the seventeen years you had with him."

"Twelve years," Robert abruptly corrected. "I wasn't alive for the first five years of his life."

"Don't be a smartass," Stan replied. "You know what I mean." Robert gazed downward, a little embarrassed. "Look," Stan continued, "I know it's hard, son, but you can't keep dwelling on the past. It's not healthy to—"

Before he could finish, Robert started for the door, but his father stopped him with a strong grip on his shoulder. Robert peered up, tears welling in his eyes, and Stan decided to let him go. "You take what you need from my box," he generously offered, "and no more than that. And you finish up this little project of yours. Fix up your bike if you want to, but you're not taking it up that godforsaken mountain, do you understand me?"

"Yes, sir," Robert quietly replied, though his father's ears detected a mocking tone. Robert moved past his father and out the door.

Down the hall, Stan could hear Robert's bedroom door slam shut. Standing by himself, he gazed across his lonely, tiny room until his weary eyes settled on a photo of happier times, taped to his work desk: Danny holding up his first-place ribbon at the school's science fair.

6

SECOND FLASHBACK

There were so many colorful streamers streaking across the high-school gymnasium's ceiling that one could be forgiven for thinking it was a pep rally and not a science fair. In fact, due to a few careless decorators, some streamers hung so low that they obscured the experiments themselves. There were the typical projects every adolescent tries their hand at, regardless of their aptitude—or interest—in science: electricity, weather, convection, even the occasional vinegar-and-baking-soda-spewing volcano that belonged more at an elementary-school science fair than one involving seventeen-year-olds like Danny.

This was Danny's third fair in as many years at his school, and he hadn't placed in any of them, not even "a lousy bronze," as his father liked to say. Similar to his father, Danny had always had a fascination with scientific gadgets and inventing things, and his latest was a small turbocharged engine for his dirt bike, which increased its speed just over the legal limit in a matter of seconds after pushing a certain button. He had to keep the engine small enough to still fit on the back of his motorbike and not be too cumbersome or heavy, or he could easily lose control while riding it. Because of its small stature, the increased rate of speed it gave the bike didn't last very long. Still, that small speed burst was a sight to behold and could extricate the bike out of a number of tight spots.

Of course, Danny couldn't exactly demonstrate his motorbike boosting to sixty miles per hour in five seconds on the gym floor, lest there would be a nasty cleanup for old man Caruso, the school's trusty long-time janitor. He had to use his dad's handy Minolta video camera to record the boost on his home's suburban street, and his father was only too happy to oblige. Danny reminded Stan of his younger self during more hopeful days, when the world was right in front of him and all he had to do was lean in, reach out, and take it.

Stan even took the day off from work to escort his son to the school fair himself. Not only was he there for moral support, but he lent an authenticity to the experiment itself. He could verify that although he supplied Danny with his tools and certain materials, Danny himself did most of the work in designing and building the small turbo engine, even putting the finishing touches like painting it cherry red to match the paint job of his bike's hard body.

His father was particularly proud of the button installation that initiated the boost; to him, it was almost like science fiction. It reminded him of *Knight Rider*, one of Danny's favorite TV shows. Whenever the title character, Michael Knight, played by campy-acting king David Hasselhoff, was in a jam driving his specialized Pontiac Firebird, he would command the highly advanced car to "turbo boost" itself out of the dangerous situation. In almost every episode, it worked, and his father wondered why Michael didn't simply use the turbo boost button at the start of each chase instead of as a last resort. Then again, if he did, each episode would be half as long.

Though Danny had street-tested his prized machine with its modified engine—after clearing a path, of course—he still had yet to test it on the ultimate challenge: Danger Peak. Scaling that mountain on his bike was the final goal he had set for himself, and the engine was merely a stepping stone toward it.

The fair's judge, Dr. Forrest Howard, was the school's award-winning science teacher, whose own wacky experiments, such as electric flypaper, landed him a photo op or two in the town's local newspaper every year. Though he liked to be addressed as "Doctor," no one exactly knew what he was a doctor *of*. He usually strode up and down the rows of boxy exhibits with an air of pretension that was a mixture of confidence and condescension, and this year was no different. He spoke little, but if he stood before you with his clipboard and pocket pen and smiled, you knew you were on the right track. If, on the other hand, he simply upturned his nose and sniffed, as if he detected someone's week-old egg-salad sandwich rotting in the school cafeteria down the hall, you knew you were in trouble. There would be no gold, no silver, not even, as Stan oft described it, "a lousy bronze."

Dr. Howard dressed not only like he was from another decade; it was like he was from another galaxy. He was often seen wearing a bright-orange bow tie, tall black boots, a long white lab coat, old oil-stained pants, and dark rubber gloves. Except for his glasses, all he needed was a white fright wig, and he could easily pass as Dr. Emmett Brown from the film *Back to the Future*. Danny sometimes wondered if he purposefully modeled his look on that crazy character. He always appeared like he was either just finishing an experiment or about to dive headfirst into one. Self-conscious of this fact and vexed by the disbelieving stares from passersby, he was already armed with a quip if a brave, though rebellious, student called him out on it: "My dear boy" (or girl, as the case could be), "all of us are continuously conducting an experiment. It's an experiment called life."

Dr. Howard had seen almost all of the students' displays, and his favorite seemed to be one featuring a solar-powered lightbulb, but Danny was curious as to how legitimate the experiment was. After all, the bulb was blazing hot white light while it was indoors with nary a sunray in sight. Also, Harry Stetson, the so-called inventor of the lightbulb, was known more for athletics and was a C+ student at best, not exactly the school's scientific brainiac.

At last, Dr. Howard marched toward Danny's experiment—the final one of the fair—and, being relatively tall at over six feet and the streamers hanging so low, irritatedly swatted the rainbow-colored ribbons from his face like the pesky, persistent flies that inspired him to create his electrified flypaper in the first place. After he made his way to Danny's display, complete with a giant poster board detailing the schematics of the engine and a "Motorbike of the Future!" banner adorning the top, Dr. Howard made his usual judging maneuvers. His eyes traveled the length of the display from top to bottom as if he were eyeing a leggy fashion model or a freshly minted Ferrari straight off the assembly line. To Dr. Howard, science was also part art, and presentation was almost as key to winning the competition as the function of the experiment itself.

"What does it do?" he finally asked.

Before Danny could answer, his father intervened. "Well, you see, my son—"

Then it was Dr. Howard's turn to interrupt. "Ah, I'd prefer the *student* to answer, if you don't mind," he said, peering suspiciously at Stan.

Danny didn't know how to react since he didn't receive Dr. Howard's trademark smile or nose sniff, so he just began babbling, attempting to answer his question as fast as possible as if the science fair were a timed test. "My motorbike is my life, Dr. Howard, only it wasn't fast enough. Until now." He gestured toward the schematic diagram to his right. "I've been working on this turbocharged engine all school year, but I finally got the modifications right. It gives a turbo boost to my dirt bike at a speed of approximately sixty miles per hour in under five seconds."

"A turbo boost?" Dr. Howard asked, cocking his left eyebrow.

"Yes, that's correct," Danny answered.

"Like *Knight Rider*?"

"Exactly!" Danny's father eagerly chimed in and was about to continue but, after receiving a disapproving glare from the good doctor, thought better of it and backed down. Danny was just stunned to discover Dr. Howard was actually familiar with a regular TV show like *Knight Rider*. He thought he only watched a steady diet of *Nova* documentaries.

"That's quite impressive," Dr. Howard finally said after turning his gaze back to Danny.

"Thanks!" he excitedly replied.

"And also *dangerous*," Dr. Howard added.

"Mr. Howard—" Danny began.

"*Doctor* Howard," he corrected.

"Right," Danny said. "*Doctor*. With all due respect, I've been riding my bike for years and have become quite an expert. I've even competed in several motocross events."

Dr. Howard began impatiently clicking his pen at his side, and the message was unmistakably clear to Danny: wrap it up.

"Anyway, I feel I've invented one of the fastest dirt bikes in the country."

"Do you have proof of this?" the doctor asked. "Remember, every scientist needs proof to back up his theories."

"Yes, I do," Danny answered, pressing "play" on the VCR he had brought to the fair. Then the small TV perched above played a short video of Danny riding his bike down the block.

"I took the video with my trusty Minolta," his father announced with prideful eyes. "You know, I'm also somewhat of an inventor myself. I—" Another glare from Dr. Howard, and Stan's story was done.

Danny attempted damage control. "Dad, you're distracting him. Just let him watch the video."

Dr. Howard did so, and as the tiny, grainy image of Danny in the video pressed a button on the bonnet of his bike, he suddenly jerked back with the front wheel in the air as an ear-splitting peal pierced the miniature TV's tinny speakers. Danny zoomed like a bat out of hell past his dad holding the camera and then out of the frame.

Now Dr. Howard raised *both* eyebrows. It was his highest praise. And, to prove the point, he quickly jotted something down on his clipboard and then walked nearby to Harry Stetson's solar-powered light-bulb. "Mr. Stetson," he droned in his low, mellifluous pipes, "the next time you want to sell me the idea of a solar-powered lightbulb, make sure your Duracell isn't showing." And with that, he reached underneath the experiment's table and unplugged a large Duracell battery, which immediately extinguished the hot white light of the bulb. Now Harry's face was hot and white—in humiliation.

He then walked back to Danny's experiment, and after searching one of the pockets of his voluminous lab coat, he pulled out a large blue ribbon. As he reached out to Danny, it was oddly reminiscent of the pre-prom tradition of pinning a corsage on your date.

"For you," he offered, pinning the ribbon on Danny's lapel.

Grinning like a jolly idiot, Danny didn't know what to say except, "Thank you!"

Before he left, Dr. Howard leaned over and, winking, suggested, "Next time, wear a helmet."

"Will do," Danny said as his father burst into applause. A few students and their mentors nearby joined reluctantly, in a haze of jealousy, with Harry acting as the center of the envious storm. Dr. Howard smiled and strode past the next project adjacent to Danny's, something about improving traffic patterns, ready to award the final two ribbons in the competition.

Stan hugged his son tightly and whispered conspiratorially into his ear, "This ain't no lousy bronze, boy." Then, taking his disposable pocket camera out of his coat, he offered, "Here, let me take a picture." Positioning himself in front of his son and bursting with pride, Stan clicked the camera's button as Danny held up the ribbon and flashed one of his famously warm smiles.

After the photo, his smile lingered until a thought struck his mind and deflated his smirk. "I wish Robert was here," he said.

7

DR. HOWARD'S CLASS

Technology class was Robert's least favorite, but it wasn't because of the subject matter. Like his father and brother before him, he loved experimenting with gadgets and gizmos and trying to invent his way out of a problem like MacGyver. The real issue was the teacher: a certain Dr. Forrest Howard. The cocky, pompous authoritarian ruled over his classroom like a dictator surveying his miniature kingdom, and it didn't even comfort Robert that he had awarded his brother a first-place ribbon in last year's science fair.

Unfortunately for Dr. Howard, but fortunately for his students, his entire authority stretched to just five desks wide by four desks long. Robert was smack dab in the middle, next to his best buds, Chris and Rinnie, who were in the middle of one of their inane discussions.

"What kind of name is Rinnie anyway?" Chris whispered to Rinnie.

"It's short for Rinniginald." Rinnie was greeted with a blank stare.

"What?" Chris asked, dumbfounded.

Attempting to help, Robert added, "Rinniginald isn't a name!"

"Tell that to my parents," Rinnie bemoaned, glumly looking at his desk.

Chris shrugged his shoulders. "Well, I guess it could be worse," he began, giggling. "It could be short for Regina." Robert joined his laughter as Rinnie simply blushed, hoping the nearby girls didn't overhear their conversation.

"Oh, you're a regular member of the Har-dee Har-Har Boys," he said.

"Quiet, you three!" Dr. Howard admonished from the front of the room, where he was demonstrating the internal workings of a standard gearbox.

"Yeah," Rinnie admonished his friends, "keep it down."

"He was talking to *all* of us," Chris interjected.

"No, he wasn't."

"He said 'you three,'" Chris said, even louder. "I know you know how to count."

"This isn't math class," Rinnie said just as Dr. Howard spun around to point a crooked digit toward the wayward trio.

"That's it! I'm separating you three," he warned.

"You see?" Chris whispered to Rinnie. "He said 'three.'"

"I said 'enough'!" their professor continued. "Christopher, go to the empty desk in the back row." Rinnie laughed mockingly in his direction until Dr. Howard's next seat reassignment. "Rinnie, move to the empty desk in the front row." Now it was Chris's turn to laugh. "Finally, Robert, head to the supply closet."

Robert's eyes widened like window shutters. Just about everyone in Dr. Howard's class had at one time or another been sent to his supply closet, which was more like a small room than a closet. There, his teacher stored all the leftover machine parts he couldn't fit either in his home or classroom since he was usually juggling five or six inventions. Despite it being only late October, Robert was one of the last few who hadn't been sent to the dreaded place of punishment, and even though he was mildly curious about what kind of knickknacks his teacher had in storage, he was in no mood to spend the rest of his class time in a darkened, claustrophobic space. It was humiliating, like they were still in early grade school, not junior high.

"Mr. Howard?" Robert began his plea.

"*Doctor* Howard," the teacher pretentiously corrected his student, as was his wont.

"Sorry, Doc . . . I mean Doctor," Robert stammered. "Would it be okay if I just stayed out here with everyone else? You can still send me to another seat away from my friends—"

"I'm your teacher," Dr. Howard cut Robert off,

"and, therefore, *I* will tell *you* what to do, not the other way around. Besides, I don't believe I've ever assigned you the closet before, so it's your turn. It's only fair."

Robert rolled his eyes at Dr. Howard's idea of what constituted "fair," but the teacher caught this snotty gesture and shot him a nastier look than his father ever did, which was enough to not only send a shiver down Robert's spine, but he sprang from his desk toward the open door of the supply closet.

"Yes, sir," he said, passing the frustrated educator.

"*Doctor,*" he once again corrected.

Robert almost flew off the handle, thinking, *"Sir" isn't respectable enough for ya?* but thought better of uttering it out loud for the classroom—and, particularly, Dr. Howard—to hear. Robert dutifully marched into that damp, musty closet like a good soldier, and for an extra dose of embarrassment, Dr. Howard closed the door and locked it with a key from one of his many lab coat pockets. Robert thought he heard some murmured laughter from just beyond the door, along with Dr. Howard instructing them to quiet down, but he decided it was better not to focus on such things. That way of thinking only leads to madness, he reasoned.

Since he couldn't exactly hear Dr. Howard's lesson anymore, Robert decided that his forceful imprisonment just might be a blessing in disguise, and with nothing else to do, he began exploring row after row of the mechanical toys and trinkets lining the closet's shelves: broken beakers, half a robotic arm with a silvery metallic claw for a hand, miniature hole-filled tires . . . Robert wondered why he bothered to keep any of this junk.

Then he spied something at the end of the closet, tucked away in the bottom corner. Like the Ark of the Covenant from the movie *Raiders of the Lost Ark*, it appeared as if it was not meant to be disturbed, yet it seemed to call his name all the same. A green blanket was half concealing it, but he almost recognized the lettering underneath. All he could make out were the letters T-U-R. His face widening with astonished recognition, Robert raced over to the object to whisk the blanket off and read the rest of the word: TURBO.

It was Danny's turbocharger.

8

BACK IN THE TREEHOUSE

"But I thought the turbocharger was destroyed!" Rinnie told the gang at their clubhouse meeting after school in Robert's treehouse. He had to raise his voice over the radio to be heard. The chorus of Martika's "Toy Soldiers" was blasting out of the tiny speakers like marching orders—"Step by step! Heart to heart!"—and Robert reached over to turn the volume down. After he twisted the knob to the appropriate level, Rinnie continued. "You know, after the boulder hit your brother's bike and killed—"

"Rinnie!" Chris admonished, shaking his head. "Jesus, king of sensitivity over here."

"Not sure what you mean," Rinnie replied, clueless as always, and retreated back into his *Nintendo Power.*

"It's okay," Robert lied. Then, attempting to

explain, "They found the bike in pieces after that boulder hit, but the turbocharger must have been one of the parts that remained intact. Somehow Dr. Howard got a hold of it and swiped it."

Always the logic-filled detective of their little club, Chris offered an alternative explanation. "Or repaired the leftover parts himself," he said. "He has the know-how to do it, and besides, didn't he award your brother the first-place ribbon in last year's science fair for it?"

"Right," Robert agreed, rubbing his chin in thought.

"He must've been pretty impressed with it to want to steal it," Chris reasoned.

"Or jealous," Robert said. "I mean none of his inventions ever seems to work, and my seventeen-year-old brother beat him at his own game."

Suddenly, Rinnie poked his porcine head from behind his magazine as if he were playing peek-a-boo.

"Isn't it illegal to remove evidence from the scene of an accident?" Rinnie asked like a wide-eyed child.

"Yep," Chris confirmed, remembering a similar detail in an episode of *Miami Vice*, his favorite TV show.

"I guess that makes Mr. Howard a criminal," Robert said.

"*Doctor* Howard," Chris mocked in their teacher's snobby voice. Besides being an armchair detective, Chris was also the resident impressionist of the group. Of the three, he had an uncanny gift for mimicking other people's voices, especially those they didn't like.

They laughed at Chris's impression of their conceited teacher just as Robert's mother called her son down for dinner.

"You better go, Rob," Rinnie warned, finally placing his *Nintendo Power* down on the small pile in the corner, "before your mom has a conniption fit."

"But aren't we going to do something about this?" Robert asked.

"What *can* we do?" Chris wondered aloud, helpless.

Without hesitating, Robert gave the gang his answer. "We go into that closet tomorrow and take it."

Chris and Rinnie simply looked at each other, dumbfounded, and then turned their attention back to their leader. "*What?*" they both exclaimed.

"It's only right," Robert replied, somewhat pretentiously. "It was my brother's invention after all. We already acknowledged that Howard stole it."

"*Doctor—*" Chris began.

"Stop that!" Robert cut him off, annoyed.

"Robby!" Robert's mother once again called just outside the treehouse, her tone increasingly irritated. "Come eat your dinner before it gets cold! I made your favorite: meatloaf and lima beans!"

"You like lima beans?" Rinnie asked in a disbelieving tone.

"No!" Robert protested a little too loudly, blushing.

"Then why did—"

"It's not important!"

"Robby!"

"Coming!" Robert fired back at his mom, getting up. "Listen, I gotta go. But you two distract Dr. Howard after class tomorrow while I go swipe the charger that he swiped from my brother." He was talking so fast it reminded Chris of the speed-talking Micro Machines pitchman on TV.

"Distract him?" Chris asked, also getting up and heading toward the trap door in the center of the floor that led to the tree trunk, with Rinnie right behind him. "How?"

"I don't know," Robert admitted, opening the wooden trapdoor. "*You're* the detective. Think of something."

THE ADVENTURE BEGINS

Dr. Howard's class normally seemed long to Robert, Chris, and Rinnie, but that afternoon, it felt especially interminable. The teacher had graciously allowed the three to sit back together again after a strict warning at the start of class, and for the most part, they remained quiet. But throughout, Robert nervously drummed his fingers on his desk, Chris kept anxiously darting his eyes back and forth to survey the room, and Rinnie impatiently doodled winged dragons, unicorns, and other favorite mythical beasts in his technology notebook when he should have been taking down the latest notes.

Occasionally, they would eye the oval clock mounted high on the wall next to the chalkboard on the far end of the room, and Dr. Howard always took that as a sign of disrespect since it was clear they weren't paying attention to his lecture and couldn't wait for his class to end. Usually, that would be enough for a punishment, but after yesterday's fiasco, he figured they were disciplined enough—for now.

Eventually, Robert tracked the movement of Chris's wild eyes, which kept ping-ponging between the supply closet and classroom door, and Robert gave him a quizzical look. Chris didn't respond, not understanding his point. Not wanting to talk out of turn again like yesterday, Robert instead borrowed the old tried-and-true school ritual of note passing. Carefully, slowly, and as quietly as possible, Robert tore off the corner of one of the pages in his notebook, scribbled down a message, folded it, and passed it to Chris next to him when their teacher's back was turned. Chris eagerly opened it: "What are you doing? Your eyes look crazy!"

As was the custom, Chris scrawled his reply on the opposite side of the original message, and judging by how long it was taking, it was clear he had more to say than Robert. He then passed the note back just as Dr. Howard turned around. Robert immediately covered the paper with his folded hands and stared intently at his teacher as supposed proof of his concentration on the lecture. It was almost a parody of how a student was supposed to act, and again, Dr. Howard was going to call him out for it, but he had wasted enough time the day before punishing him and had too much work to get through that day. Robert unfolded Chris's note: "I'm trying to measure the distance between the closet and classroom door when we make our escape. I hope we have enough time to give him the slip."

Robert tried to stifle a chuckle. *Chris really is a detective sometimes*, he thought. It felt like they were in a heist movie. He couldn't believe they were actually going to do this and wondered if they would get away with it. He felt like a little kid again, as if he were back in his yard with Danny playing cops and robbers with plastic water guns and bandanas. He was going to write a response when the bell rang. He was having so much fun passing notes that he completely forgot to keep track of the clock.

"Alright, class," Dr. Howard announced, resignedly placing his worn-down chalk back on the chalkboard's lower shelf. "You've suffered enough." The class collectively marveled at their teacher's uncharacteristic self-awareness, an audible gasp almost escaping their lips. Then they all excitedly filed out the door. All except three, that is.

Dr. Howard himself was about to leave to reward himself with a coffee when the gang set their plan in action. Chris and Rinnie got up from their desks and prepared to walk toward the professor as Robert pretended to gather his belongings at his desk. An astute teacher probably would have noticed that it doesn't take several minutes just to place one notebook in a schoolbag and zip it up, but Dr. Howard wasn't your average teacher who cared for such things, and that's exactly what the Wild Boars were counting on.

What Robert was actually doing was emptying his backpack and cramming all his books and supplies into his technology desk. Luckily for them, it was their last class of the day, so he wasn't going to need his books anyway. Robert managed to fit the last fat textbook—math, natch—into the desk's opening when several pens spilled out from the stuffing and clacked loudly on the floor. *Now* Dr. Howard was paying attention. He spun around in Robert's direction just as Chris and Rinnie approached him at the front of the room.

"Excuse me!" Chris began, grabbing Dr. Howard's arm. Dr. Howard peevishly peered down at Chris's hand, his eyes seemingly saying, "How *dare* you touch me!" Noticing this, Chris immediately withdrew his hand. "May we have a word with you?" he asked.

Now Dr. Howard fully turned toward Chris and Rinnie as Robert cautiously snuck behind him and quietly entered the supply closet.

"A *word*?" he asked Chris suspiciously. He may not have always paid attention to his students' antics, but he also knew they didn't exactly talk like reporters from the 1940s either.

"What my good friend Chris here means," Rinnie added helpfully but, as usual, stumbling all over himself, "is that we were really impressed with your lecture today and wanted to know if you were willing to elucidate and extrapolate your point further."

Chris rolled his eyes. He would've slapped his forehead in painful frustration if their teacher wasn't directly in front of them. "'Elucidate and extrapolate'?"

This wasn't the common vernacular of a pair of thirteen-year-olds. Clearly, Rinnie was overcompensating to impress their teacher. Just as clearly, Dr. Howard was onto their game.

"Really?" he asked. Flashing a large set of shiny, shark-like teeth, Dr. Howard moved in for the kill. "And why don't you *elucidate* to me your favorite part of my lecture?"

"Uh, favorite part?" Rinnie asked, glancing at Chris for a lifeline.

"Yes," Dr. Howard replied. "In fact, can you even remember the topic of the lecture?"

Chris gulped like a doomed villain from a Bugs Bunny cartoon. He felt like he was hovering in midair over a bottomless canyon. All that was missing was a sign reading "Help!" He had spent all that time worrying about the distance between the closet and classroom doors that he hadn't bothered paying attention to his teacher's lecture.

"Perhaps," the doctor continued, closing the classroom door in front of them with an impish smirk twisting his gaunt face, "you boys need to stay after class for extra help."

"Uhhh," Chris panicked, looking at Rinnie helplessly. "I've got nothin'."

Crash! Suddenly, a loud smashing sound was heard from the supply closet, and Dr. Howard quickly spun around and walked in its direction.

"What the devil was *that*?" he asked.

"Um," Rinnie adlibbed, "our crushed hopes for

getting away with this?" *Now* Chris slapped his forehead.

Dr. Howard had had enough. He stormed angrily into the supply closet, but it was too dark to see. After he flicked on the adjacent light switch, the first thing greeting his eyes was a tray of broken test tubes splayed on the floor. Chris and Rinnie swiftly sidled up beside their teacher to peer into the closet. Robert was nowhere to be found.

"Phew!" Rinnie sighed exasperatedly.

"Would you shut up?" Chris whispered, ribbing him with his elbow. Dr. Howard bent to the floor to pick up one of the broken pieces from his precious test tube collection. Chris thought he saw a tear forming behind the man's glasses.

"Who did this?" he asked no one in particular.

Chris could see Rinnie formulating a response, the gears practically grinding in his brain, and he worried his friend would fall back on his oft-used excuse that he would deliver time and time again in years past at sleepovers at his house whenever they woke up Rinnie's mother.

Don't say a mouse, don't say a mouse, don't say a mouse, Chris thought.

On cue, Rinnie asked, "A mouse?" Chris slapped his forehead again as Dr. Howard bent down to get in Rinnie's face.

"That must've been some mouse," he said.

"It'll chomp your skull off, dude."

"Mice aren't big enough to knock over a tray of test

tubes," Dr. Howard concluded. "Besides," he snarled, "I run a clean ship in this classroom. The only vermin currently occupying it are you gentlemen." Now Chris was glad he missed Dr. Howard's lecture because it seemed he was getting a completely new one. "Boys," their teacher continued with a tone of suspicion, "I don't know what you're up to, but one way or another, I'm going to find—"

"Ah-choo!" came from the back of the closet. Dr. Howard strode toward the sound, which appeared to be coming from just behind a green blanket—a *dusty* green blanket. Like a magician briskly removing a tablecloth without disturbing the contents on top, Dr. Howard whisked the blanket away and revealed what was hiding underneath. There was Robert, huddled in a ball and clutching his backpack with his brother's beloved turbocharger inside. He flashed a sheepish smile and weakly waved back at his astonished professor.

"And for my next trick," Dr. Howard announced. Robert swallowed hard. "I'm going to make you boys disappear."

10

THE TURBOCHARGER

"Robert Kin," Dr. Howard began, "what the hell are you doing here?"

Immediately, Rinnie shook his head and clucked his tongue in disapproval. "It's not nice to swear, Mr. Howard," he scolded as if *he* were the teacher in this situation.

"*Doctor*," the man muttered under his breath. Then, turning to Robert again, he added, "Well? I'm waiting."

Robert opened his mouth, but no words came. Dr. Howard crossed his arms and drummed his fingers impatiently on his elbows.

Finally, Chris came to Robert's rescue. "He was just interested in getting a closer look at your amazing invention, the electric flypaper," he said, grabbing a nearby carton off the shelf and throwing it into Robert's hands.

Dr. Howard cocked an eyebrow. "Is that true, Robert?"

"Uh, yeah," Robert said, slowly getting up off the floor.

"Then what were you doing hiding in the corner, and why did you break my test tubes?"

"It was an accident," Robert explained. "As I was looking for the flypaper, I accidentally knocked them over, and then when I heard you coming, I was so embarrassed, I tried to hide."

"Hmph," the doctor snorted. "You should've just put on the light. Seeing as how you have great taste in inventions—*and* inventors—I'm letting you off with a warning this time. Now get out of here before I change my mind."

"Yeah," Rinnie joked, "come out of the closet, Robert."

"All of you," Dr. Howard barked. "Get out of my classroom!"

The three did as they were told, but as Robert passed, Dr. Howard noticed something peculiar: Robert's schoolbag was partly open at the top, and something familiar was jutting out of the zipper. "What is that?" he asked, tapping Robert on the shoulder.

"What's what?" Robert asked, playing dumb. Dr. Howard didn't say a word. He merely pointed to the backpack, which was opening even more as Robert shifted its contents, the weight of the turbocharger pulling the zipper down even further to expose his stolen loot.

Suddenly, Dr. Howard's eyes were ablaze. "Why," he began, "that looks like my—"

Before he could finish, Robert quickly zipped up his bag as much as he could and flew through the classroom doorway, with Rinnie and Chris following close behind.

"Later, Buster Brown!" Rinnie called as Chris rolled his eyes at the impromptu insult.

"Wait!" Dr. Howard futilely called, running into the hallway after them as fast as his fifty-year-old legs could carry him. "Stop them!" he ordered to no one in particular. Most kids in the hallway felt the same about Dr. Howard as the three students outrunning him: at best, apathy; at worst, revulsion. In other words, they were in no mood to help. In fact, one snotty student extended a leg and tripped the gangly professor, who tumbled face-first onto the hard linoleum tile of the floor.

Rinnie peered over one shoulder to see the commotion and laughed. Then, turning to his two friends running with him, he added, "Hey, guys, did you see that?"

"Not now, Rinnie," Chris instructed, choosing instead to focus on making their getaway. Rounding a corner, they could see the school's front entrance at the end of the hallway.

Robert made the mistake of turning around, only to see Dr. Howard round the corner himself a few feet behind them. Even though he couldn't run as fast as his young students, his long legs seemed to be making up the difference. Robert and Chris decided to pick up the pace, but Rinnie slowed down as he passed his dream girl.

"Hey, babe!" he called.

"It's Barbara!" she shouted back, bracing the books against her chest like a shield.

"Not now, Rinnie!" Chris once again admonished his friend.

Just then, Dr. Howard outstretched his long arm and managed to grab a few hairs off Rinnie's head. "Whoa!" Rinnie shouted as he sped up to match the speed of Robert and Chris.

Robert knew he had to take evasive action. They were only halfway down the hall, and at the rate that their teacher was gaining, they'd never make it. Robert looked down at the box of electric flypaper still in his hand. With a few deft maneuvers, he tore open the cardboard carton, unpeeled the protective covering of the flypaper, and plugged in the tiny battery pack that came included. The electric flypaper instantly buzzed to life, and before it could sting his fingers, he threw it in Dr. Howard's direction.

"Catch!" he called as it landed on Dr. Howard's face, clinging to his left cheek and singeing the flesh.

Dr. Howard stopped in his tracks, clutched his face, and bellowed, "Argh! It burns!"

"Great invention, Dr. Howard!" Rinnie called out behind him.

At least he got my title right this time, the teacher thought as he peeled the paper off, stripping some layers of skin in the process.

That bought them some time to escape through the school's main entrance. The three of them crashed through the blocky doors almost at once, bumping a few students out of the way in the process. They then raced down the stairs and headed for their dirt bikes parked against the school's bike rack. Robert frantically looked for Rinnie's bike.

"Where's your bike, Rinnie?" he asked.

"It's in the shop," he admitted.

"In the shop?" Robert repeated, thunderstruck. "Today of all days? You knew about our plan!"

"I'm sorry," he apologized. "I blew out the engine last night racing it through the woods."

"Never mind," Robert improvised. "Climb on the back of my bike with me."

As Chris wrapped his legs around his dirt bike and strapped his helmet on, Rinnie hesitated. "Hey, man," he joked to Robert, "you're a great guy and everything, but I really don't think you're my type."

Suddenly, the school doors behind them burst open, and a panting, irritated Dr. Howard shot forward through the crowd of departing students like a bullet. Since school was letting out, it was difficult to pinpoint the three students he was searching for, but hearing them argue with each other helped.

"There's Howard now," Chris warned, pointing at the staircase leading to their junior high.

"There's no time to argue," Robert told Rinnie. "Just pretend I'm Barbara and get on already!"

"Fine," Rinnie said reluctantly, planting himself on

the bike's seat behind Robert, "but you owe me a dinner."

"Guards!" Dr. Howard called to a pair of security officers on the school steps. "Get those kids!"

Robert immediately revved the engine to life as the guards bounded after them with huge, muscular strides. Chris and Robert's dirt bikes peeled away from the bike rack and out of the parking lot as the riders breathed a sigh of relief.

"We made it!" Rinnie yelled triumphantly over the roar of the engines.

"Don't break out the cake just yet," Chris warned. "Howard called the school guards on us."

"Don't worry about it," Rinnie said. "How fast can those guys be?"

As if on cue, the sound of a car siren split the air between them. The three boys turned around to see the security guards' car closing in on them.

"Very," Robert answered.

11

THE CHASE

As the security car inched closer to the three fugitives, Chris shook his head in defeat.

"Great," he scoffed. "What do we do now?"

"Go into evasive action," Robert ordered as if he were a determined star commander on a spacecraft, but there was no response from his "crew."

"Care to explain that?" Chris asked.

Robert thought about all the times he rode his bike through the piles of leaves in his street. "Just follow my lead," Robert said and intentionally began ramming into nearby garbage cans.

"What are you doing, Rob?" Rinnie, still seated behind him, asked. "Don't forget I'm on here too."

"Just watch," Robert answered with confidence as the full garbage cans tumbled behind them and dumped their dirty contents onto the guard car's hood. The driver pumped his brakes as banana peels, ripped trash bags, and other assorted debris splashed across his windshield, obscuring his view.

"Genius!" Chris enthused as he followed suit by plowing into every garbage can in sight.

"Yeah," Rinnie noted dryly, "we're lucky it was garbage day." Robert simply smiled, grateful that his plan worked.

But their excitement was short-lived. Turning his head around once more, Robert saw that the garbage distraction was only a temporary setback as the guards' car quickly gained speed and closed the distance between them.

It seemed Chris noticed too. "What now, oh fearless leader?" he asked sarcastically.

As much as the insult stung, Robert had to admit his friend had a point. After all, the guards were in a car, and he and his gang were on dirt bikes. They couldn't simply outrun them. Then again, they had two vehicles, and the guards only had one. That's when he got another brainstorm.

"Split up!" he shouted over the hum of the engines. "Take a left at this upcoming fork!"

Chris simply nodded, hoping the guards would choose to chase him. He felt it was the honorable thing to do, not only by protecting his club and its leader but also the ever-important turbocharger his leader was carrying. Obediently, Chris did as he was told and swerved his dirt bike to the left at the street's intersection. "C'mon, ya punks!" he called to the guards behind him, but they didn't take the bait.

Racing past the fork in the road, the car continued its pursuit of Robert and Rinnie, leaving Chris behind as an afterthought. Chris cursed the air as a cloud of dust erupted from the passing car.

Donning his detective hat again, Chris figured the guards decided to chase Robert because there were two kids on his bike for the price of one, or maybe they knew he had the turbocharger, but either way, they were long gone. Silently, Chris wished his friends luck and knew they would rendezvous later at a future club meeting.

"They're still coming!" Rinnie warned Robert, tapping him from behind on his shoulder.

"I know, Rinnie," he said. "There's only one thing left to do. We need to use the turbocharger. I brought a screwdriver just in case of an emergency, and this sure looks like one."

"Where is it?" Rinnie asked, still having to yell over the whine of the engines from both their bike and the guards' car.

"It's in the secret compartment behind you," Robert called.

Rinnie frantically looked behind him but only saw the rear tire. "I don't see it!" he shouted.

Robert then realized there was less seat space with Rinnie sitting behind him. "You're sitting on it," he told Rinnie. "You're going to have to get up to open it."

"What?" Rinnie asked in frustration.

Suddenly, they heard a bullhorn blaring from the guard car directly behind them. "Pull the bike over, boys!"

Robert turned around to see one of the guards was leaning out the passenger-side window and screaming into a bullhorn.

"Just do it, Rinnie!" Robert ordered. "There isn't time!"

"Why does this stuff always happen to me?" Rinnie wondered in vain. Psyching himself up, he took two deep breaths and clenched his legs tighter around the bike's frame. Then he placed one hand on top of Robert's shoulder and slowly lifted himself off the seat and twisted his body to see the small compartment door he had been sitting on. Using his free hand, Rinnie began to open the compartment door when the bike hit a pothole in the road, jerking the vehicle upward and making Rinnie lose his balance. Almost falling off the bike, he tightened his grip on Robert's shoulder.

"Thanks for the massage," Robert joked. "I thought you didn't think of me that way."

"Ha-ha," Rinnie sarcastically spat. "I'm glad you're having so much fun while I almost died back here."

"Did you get the screwdriver yet?"

"I'm working on it!" Once more, while holding on to Robert's shoulder for leverage, Rinnie gingerly lifted himself up and then opened the small compartment door directly beneath him. Next to a thick corded rope that was tied off to a metal flange, the orange screwdriver rattled noisily around inside the hub. "I got it!" Rinnie cheered and grabbed the tool with gusto. He held it aloft toward Robert's eyes as proof, as if he were He-Man triumphantly raising his power sword to the electrified sky.

"Great," Robert replied impatiently as his bike made another hairpin turn around a corner. "Now use it!"

Rinnie stared dopily at the suburban scenery whipping past his head. "Uh . . . for what?"

"To install the turbocharger, dingus!" Robert, at his wit's end, answered.

"Oh yeah!" Rinnie replied. Robert could almost imagine the lightbulb flashing over his head like some comic-strip panel. Rinnie carefully removed the charger from Robert's backpack and snapped it into place next to the engine, but because it wasn't screwed in yet, it wobbled violently side to side.

"Don't damage it, dude," Robert cautioned. "My brother made it."

"Don't worry, man," Rinnie responded. Then, "Whoops!"

"'Whoops' what?" Robert asked in astonishment.

"Just kidding," his friend admitted.

Robert simply shook his head and replied with his favorite tongue twister. "Cut the comedy, comedian, and quit clownin'!"

"Who's joking now?" Rinnie criticized as he began fiddling with the two wires attached to the front of the charger. "What do I do with these wires?"

"Isn't it obvious?" Robert asked. "Red wire to red plug, blue wire to blue plug, or are you colorblind too?"

"Sorry I'm not as technical-minded as you or Chris," Rinnie stated.

"How did you put your bike together, then?" Robert asked.

"My dad did most of the work," Rinnie confessed. "Okay, all of it."

"Now you tell me," Robert said as Rinnie plugged the wires in.

"Okay, they're in, but nothing's happening."

"The charger needs to be stable to work," Robert explained. Then he dug four screws, each inserted into a washer, from his pants pocket. Like the Boy Scout he used to be, he always came prepared.

"Here," he said, offering Rinnie one of those screw-washer combos. "Screw this into the base of the charger. Let me know when you're done, and I'll hand you the next one."

Rinnie did as he was told, in a surprisingly fluid process. For once, the Wild Boars' comic sidekick wasn't a laughingstock. Robert figured it finally dawned on Rinnie how dire their situation was.

Just then, Robert made another turn into a darkened alley only to realize, after looking ahead in the distance, that it was a dead end. The sole contents were piles of broken crates leaning against a brick wall. Despite the chill autumnal air blowing past his brown locks, Robert's forehead broke into a panicked sweat.

"You better hurry up," he warned Rinnie. "We're running out of time . . . and space!" He pointed to the brick wall quickly advancing toward their vehicle.

Rinnie looked up and almost passed out. "Alright," he shouted above the rushing wind and roar of the engine, "one more to go." After snapping the last screw in and hastily tightening it with the screwdriver, he triumphantly announced, "I did it!"

"Yes!" Robert cheered, waiting for the inevitable burst of speed . . . which didn't come. Meanwhile, the wall at the end of the alleyway was rapidly approaching. "What happened?" he asked Rinnie.

"I dunno," Rinnie answered. "Maybe it's broke."

"Well, did you turn it *on*?" Robert asked.

"You didn't tell me I had to turn it on," Rinnie protested. If he could, Robert would've turned around to strangle his friend. "Where is it?"

"It's on the bottom. A small round button."

"I can't see it!" Rinnie shouted, terror rising in his voice.

"Feel for it," Robert instructed.

Rinnie did so but, in the process, accidentally dropped the screwdriver. "I dropped your screwdriver," he admitted, abashed.

"Don't worry about it," Robert reassured him. "That's not important now. Just push the button."

Obeying his group's leader, Rinnie finally found the

button, and his forefinger firmly pressed down on it. "I did it!" Rinnie cheered for what seemed like the umpteenth time.

Grinning from ear to ear, Robert wrapped his fingers tightly around his bike's handlebars and braced for the thrust of the turbo boost, but his smile withered as the engine sputtered. Nothing was happening. Robert reasoned to himself that the turbocharger must have been sitting on Dr. Howard's dusty shelf for too long and was most likely out of commission.

Robert gazed at the upcoming dead end with a sense of doom; it was now only several dozen feet away from them. This was it: The wall. The guards' car. The failed engine. It was all a recipe for disaster. Robert's bottom lip quivered as he felt Rinnie's hands slip from his torso. Above the roar of the engine, Robert could hear Rinnie openly weeping. *Always a coward*, Robert thought, *until the end.*

"Start, darn ya, start!" Robert yelled. In desperate frustration, he swiftly kicked the engine behind him with his right foot.

Vroom!

Just as their bike was about to slam into the brick wall, the turbocharger roared to life and sent a surge of electrified energy into the tiny engine. The bike popped a wheelie as Rinnie lost his grip and fell off. As the bike ramped up speed, Robert turned his head to see Rinnie holding on to the secret compartment's rope for dear life.

"Hold on!" Robert excitedly—and perhaps

unnecessarily—ordered as he gripped the handlebars even more strongly. The engine hummed like a turbo-jet as Robert aimed for a broken crate shaped like a ramp. The bike blasted across the ramp and popped over the wall, with a hapless Rinnie dangling danger-ously behind and screaming his head off. It was safe to say no rollercoaster he had been on could compete with this trip.

As the tires noisily scraped the top of the wall, leaving a flaming crisscross mark imprinted on the red bricks like the time-traveling DeLorean in *Back to the Future*, a shower of sparks blasted from the bike's tailpipe and blanketed the guard car's windshield in an impromptu fireworks display, blinding their line of sight. Shouting in dismay, the driver jerked the steering wheel to the left and slammed the brakes as the car violently screeched to a halt, just missing the brick wall by a few feet.

At least now Robert knew the turbocharger worked.

12

TROUBLE AT HOME

"Do anything interesting today?" Donna innocently asked her son at dinner that night while swallowing another piece of her famous roast beef. Robert wasn't sure how to answer.

"Well, speak up, boy," Stan scolded. "Your mother asked you a question."

Robert took a long slug of root beer, clearly stalling for time. It was even obvious to his mom. "Oh, same ol' same ol'," Robert finally lied while carefully slicing his beef with a serrated knife.

"What's that supposed to mean?" Stan asked.

"I hung out with Chris and Rinnie after school," Robert answered. "That's why I was late."

Stan clucked his tongue in between munching his corn niblets. "I told you I don't like you hanging out with those losers," he said, pointing his knife at

Robert. If Robert didn't know any better, he would have considered it a threat.

"Stan, put the knife down," Donna calmly ordered.

"What?" he asked, feigning surprise with a wicked smirk. "I wasn't going to kill him with it. Just cut him a little."

"Stan!" she shouted.

"Relax, Donna," he said, "it's a joke."

"Well," she began, delicately wiping her bottom lip with a cloth napkin, "it wasn't funny at all."

"That's okay," Robert offered. "I'm used to his abuse." Outside the house, you could hear some children laughing as they passed, a lonely dog howling uselessly at the moon, and even a faint police siren in the distance, but it was quiet as a tomb inside that dining room.

"What did you say?" Stan asked, breaking the quiet with an incredulous tenor in his voice. Now Robert was really at a loss for words. He glanced toward his mother for a lifeline, but even she seemed to abandon her son. Before Stan could repeat his question, the doorbell rang.

"Saved by the bell," Stan huffed and then rose from the table to answer the door. After he left the table, Donna shot her son a discouraging look.

"What?" Robert asked.

"I know your father can be rough around the edges," she began, "but he *is* your father, and you shouldn't talk to him that way."

"So he can talk to me like trash, but I can't defend

myself?" he asked as he heard his father open the front door in the adjacent hallway.

"That's not what I'm saying," she said.

"Then what *are* you saying?"

Before she could answer, Robert heard his father's voice rise with concern. "What's this all about, Officers?" Stan asked. Upon hearing the word *officers*, Robert felt his heart fall into the ocean of his stomach. Even his mother furrowed her brow in the direction of the front door. Robert was about to retreat to his bedroom when he heard his father yell, "Robert, get over here now!"

Robert slowly did as he was told, and although his home's foyer was next to the dining room, he felt like he were walking the green mile to the electric chair.

Entering the hallway that led to the door, he recognized the two men in the entranceway immediately, even with his father's hulking frame partially obscuring the view. They were the two school guards who had chased him and his friends that afternoon. His father spun around in Robert's direction and asked sarcastically, "Do these gentlemen look familiar to you?"

Robert decided to play dumb. "I've never seen them before in my life."

"Alright, Robert," the taller guard began, calling his bluff, "where is it?"

"Where's what?" Robert asked.

With one hand still holding the door open, Stan clenched his left fist by his side. "Robert," he started, "you may be dumb, but you're not *that* dumb."

"The turbocharger," the smaller guard explained, finally speaking up. "The one you stole? Where is it?"

Robert was defiant. "I didn't steal anything!" he rebuked. In a way, it wasn't far from the truth, Robert reasoned to himself, since the charger rightfully belonged to its owner and inventor: his brother.

Now Donna was standing directly behind Robert, almost like a prizefighter's trainer in the boxing ring. "If he says it wasn't him, I believe him," she said. "Maybe it was his friends Chris and Rinnie." Just like his father, Donna had never trusted them.

Stan looked Robert straight in the eyes, giving him one last chance to redeem himself. "Robert, answer the men. Did you take the turbocharger or not?"

Robert planted his feet firmly to the floor as if they were rooted to the linoleum itself. "I didn't," he said. "I'm not lying."

"Well, you know what *doesn't* lie?" a familiar voice floated almost musically over the shoulders of the two guards. "A photograph." Instantly, Dr. Howard appeared out of the shadows with a Polaroid picture in his hand. A white gauzy bandage was wrapped around his left cheek where the electric flypaper had struck him earlier that day. Robert noticed it immediately, and he anxiously wondered how long it would take his father to be curious about it. "The name is Dr. Forrest Howard, Robert's technology teacher," he introduced himself, extending his arm to shake hands with Stan.

"I remember," Stan replied. Glancing at his hand

after Dr. Howard released it, he realized he had slipped him the photograph like a mobster bribing a corrupt cop. As he gazed at the picture, Stan shook his head in disgust.

Needing proof herself, Donna snatched the photo from his hand. As it passed between his father and mother, Robert could clearly see the moment from his adventurous afternoon that was frozen in time: Robert, with Rinnie seated behind him, was riding away from the school on his bike, his backpack partially open and exposing the infamous turbocharger. Robert was actually impressed at the level of detail in the photo.

Almost as if he were reading Robert's mind, Dr. Howard made a formal announcement in his typically grandiloquent fashion. "A spy camera that can produce Polaroid-quality pictures," he proudly informed the small group, explaining something that no one had wondered about aloud. "One of my handy new inventions."

Suddenly, Stan's eyes turned to Dr. Howard's face, finally noticing the white bandage on the teacher's left cheek. "What happened to your face, Doctor?" he asked. Robert audibly gulped like he was Wile E. Coyote about to plummet off a cliff.

"Oh, I slipped and fell in my bathroom," Dr. Howard tersely replied, brushing the question away like an annoying gnat.

Grateful but confused as to why he was covering for him, Robert decided to worry about it later. Right now, there were more pressing matters to attend to, like the fact that his teacher was accusing him of theft in front of his two mortified parents.

Before Robert could surmise a reason for Dr. Howard's deceit, his teacher changed the subject by turning to him and announcing, practically in villainous triumph, "My dear Mr. Kin, did you really think you could outrun someone who had your home address on file at school?"

"I, I . . . uh," Robert stuttered but then simply surrendered. Even he knew there was no talking his way out of this one. Unfortunately, his teacher was right: pictures don't lie.

"Oh, Robert, how *could* you?" Donna asked, the layer of betrayal rich in her voice. Meanwhile, it took all of Stan's energy not to slap his son in front of everyone right then and there. As *his* father before him used to call it, "doling out a little corporal punishment."

"I'm sorry, Mom," he apologized, a tear forming in the corner of his eye. His mother's face fell, filled simultaneously with disappointment and empathy. Robert could see his mother's eyes wrestle with the contradictory emotions.

His father was far less sympathetic. "I'll deal with you later, son," he began, his voice trembling in anger, "but right now, just give the charger back to your teacher before he recommends expelling you."

"I don't have it anymore," Robert lied again. "I sold it."

"So soon?" Dr. Howard suspiciously asked, clearly unconvinced.

"Well, *yeah*," Robert replied in a confrontational tone as if he were saying "*duh*." "Why do you think we were riding away so fast? I had to meet with my fence." *Fence* was a term Robert had only learned the week before on one of his favorite TV programs, *Hill Street Blues*.

"How much?" the doctor asked.

"About a hundred bucks," he replied, spitting out yet another lie.

Dr. Howard blanched. "The charger was worth at least three times that," he said, astonished.

"I don't have three hundred bucks," Robert admitted.

Just then, as if coming to his rescue, Stan sighed exhaustedly. "No," he began, "but I do. Let me get my checkbook."

After Robert's father exited the foyer toward his man cave upstairs, Dr. Howard gave a stern look to Robert's mother as if she were Robert himself in class. "You know, Mrs. Kin," he began, "I believe juvenile criminal behavior such as this normally starts from the home. Have you noticed Robert acting out recently?"

Donna stitched her eyebrows together. "Frankly, Mr. Howard—" she began.

"*Doctor*," he corrected her.

"*Mr.* Howard," she continued, unfazed, "I don't believe that's any of your concern."

"When a student makes off with one of my prized possessions," he countered, "I make it my concern."

"It's not your prized possession," Robert mocked,

using air quotes on his last two words. "My brother, Danny, invented that charger, and you know it. You just swiped it because you couldn't stand the fact someone less than half your age invented something that actually works!"

"Robert!" Donna snapped, her face flushing red with embarrassment.

Ignoring the insult, Dr. Howard calmly explained, "Your brother's charger was donated to me upon his bike's destruction on Danger Peak."

"What?" Robert asked, taken aback. "That's not true!"

"It *is* true, Robert," Stan refuted, returning downstairs with a check in his hand. "Once Danny's bike was destroyed, we wanted nothing to do with the evidence. I didn't want to look at those pieces—even the mostly intact ones—for one more second. I wanted them as far away from here as possible. They only brought us bad memories." Blinking back tears, Stan then gestured toward the teacher. "Dr. Howard here expressed interest in studying the turbocharger for scientific purposes, and we donated it."

Robert shot his teacher another dirty look. Again, Dr. Howard ignored it or at least pretended not to notice.

"Wait," Robert began, confused as ever, "let me get this straight. Danny made the turbocharger, it was destroyed at Danger Peak, and you donated it to Dr. Howard?"

"We didn't want you following in your brother's

footsteps," Donna offered, her voice heavy with emotion.

"Then I stole it back," Robert continued, pacing back and forth as if he were Columbo trying to solve a labyrinthine logic puzzle, "and now you're paying him for it?"

"I was able to repair the damage after the boulder's collision that struck down your brother," Dr. Howard explained a little too matter-of-factly. "Besides, I added a few modifications to his design, which cost me a pretty penny, I must say."

"This should cover it," Stan said, handing him the check.

Dr. Howard peered down at the offering with a pleased grin. "Indeed it does."

"Well, then," Stan began, intending to conclude the awkward evening as quickly as possible, "if there's nothing else."

The doctor turned to the two security guards. For a moment, Robert had forgotten they were even there.

"We're done here," he snapped as if addressing his lapdogs. "Wait for me in the car." They nodded and, after exchanging some brief pleasantries with Robert's parents, left the porch.

"As I was explaining to your wife, Donna," he told Stan, "criminal behavior normally begins in the home. I'd keep an eye on your son if I were you."

Stan walked up to the teacher and stood nose to nose with him. "I'll discipline my son the way I want to, thank you very much," he began, "and don't ever speak to my wife like that again, do you understand?" Suddenly, the tables turned, Dr. Howard began to sweat and fidget in place. "You've got your money," Stan continued firmly, "now leave me and my family alone."

"Yes, well," a flustered Dr. Howard said, adjusting his tie. "Good day, uh, *night* to you."

"Goodbye," Stan said and then promptly closed the door in his face with a resounding thud. For a second, since they seemed to share the same enemy, Robert thought he might get away with the whole affair, until he saw his father's face turn toward him.

"You're in a *world* of trouble, Robert," he loudly announced. "Neither of us is a fan of that pompous teacher of yours, but stealing is stealing, no matter who it's from."

Still, there was a slight hint of sympathy just behind his tired eyes, though Robert reasoned it could just be the lingering memory of his brother. Robert decided to use Danny's memory to his advantage.

"How can it be stealing if Danny made it?" he asked. He thought it was a reasonable question. Apparently, he was wrong.

"I'm not explaining myself again," Stan angrily retorted. "Up to your room now! No more supper for you."

"Fine," a surly Robert answered as he retreated to his bedroom. "I don't like roast beef anyway."

"Boy, you're gonna get it!" Stan hollered after his son as he stalked up the stairs.

Robert was going to respond in kind but thought better of it and simply closed his bedroom door behind him. It had been a long day, after all.

13

THIRD FLASHBACK

Sparks flew from the metal frame of the turbocharger as Danny welded the final piece into place, lighting up the darkened garage with an eerie flicker. After months of tireless work, it seemed his master project was almost complete. Squeezing the job in the hours between dinner and bedtime, Danny and his father had worked doggedly to bring their blueprints to life. Stan was even reminded of the famous scene in *Franken-stein*, and driving the point home, he announced, "It's alive!" with a chortle in his voice.

Not quite as enthusiastic as his old man, Danny simply cracked a half-smile. "Well, not yet," he said, flipping up his welder's mask to reveal his sweaty, greasy yet handsome visage. "I still have to test it. Also, it could use a paintjob."

"What for?" his father asked.

"You know," Danny began, "to jazz it up a little."

Stan chuckled. "I didn't know you were into jazz, what with all the Pink Floyd and Led Zeppelin you keep crankin' in your bedroom."

Danny shook his head and carefully placed his welder's torch down on top of a recycling can. "You know what I mean, Dad."

"I know," he agreed, taking a sip from his can of beer. "I'm just being a smartass."

"What else is new?" Danny joked. The two laughed as the garage door leading into their home's foyer opened.

Not noticing, Stan obliviously continued their conversation. "I'm picturing a yellow lightning bolt to demonstrate how fast this baby will make your bike," he said while Danny looked up to see Robert enter the garage and close the door behind him.

"How's it going in here, guys?" Robert asked. Stan turned to his younger son, finally noticing his presence. Dressed in Spider-Man pajamas and almost ready for bed, he looked as out of place in the dirty garage as a baby in a wrestling ring. "Can I help?" he asked with hopeful eyes.

Danny opened his mouth to answer but was abruptly cut short by his father. "Get out of here, Robby!" Stan yelled impatiently. "The work we're doing here is dangerous, and you're too young."

Robert looked askance as Danny attempted to come to his defense. "Let him just hang with us for a little while, Dad," he offered. Robert smiled, knowing

Danny was always there to protect him, even from his own father.

"No way," Stan argued. "Besides, we're almost done anyway, and it's late. Kids his age should be in bed by now."

"But—" Robert protested.

"I said go," Stan ordered.

Robert looked to his older brother once more as their mother opened the door behind him. "Come on, honey," she sweetly goaded. "You heard your father. It's time to wash up for bed."

Stan took another swig of his beer while Danny looked to his younger brother and shrugged as if to say, "What can I do?"

"It's no fair," Robert grumbled childishly, turning around to exit the garage. "I never get to have any fun." His mother placed an encouraging arm around his shoulder to lead him inside the warm house.

"We'll go to the movies this weekend, buddy," Danny called to his brother's retreating shadow. "They're doing a special showing of *Star Wars*."

As soon as the garage door closed, Stan focused back on their work. "I think we're out of paint," he said, not skipping a beat from their previous conversation. "We'll go to the hardware store this Saturday."

"I'd like to see *Star Wars* with Robert though," Danny said.

"You'll go next weekend," Stan replied, taking another gulp of his beer.

"Like I told him, it's a special showing of old movies," Danny explained. "One day only."

"Christ," Stan cursed, "how many times have you boys seen that blasted movie anyway? You must've worn out the VHS tape by now."

"That's not the point, Dad," Danny argued. "It's his favorite movie, and he wasn't old enough to see it on the big screen the first time it came out like I was. I promised I'd take him."

"Well, just break that promise and make it up to him later," his father suggested.

"How?"

"I dunno," he slurred after another sip of beer, almost finishing the can. "You're smart. You invented this thing, didn't you?" He pointed at the charger, still smoking from the soldering session. "You'll think of something."

Danny shook his head and removed his gloves in disgust. "Sometimes I think you're too hard on him, Dad," he said, surprising himself with his candor.

Stan drank the last drop of beer, crumpled the can with his fingers, and then threw the empty container into the recycling bin. "Who asked you?" he challenged, his eyes narrowing.

"Nobody, but it's the truth," Danny countered, standing his ground. "Even Mom notices it."

"Leave your mother out of this," he warned, sticking a strong finger in Danny's direction.

Danny knew how his father tended to overreact

when he was drinking, so he decided to just drop it. After taking off his welder's helmet and placing it on the adjacent shelf his father had built into the garage wall, he wiped his greasy calloused hands against his torn blue jeans and motioned toward the door.

"I think that's enough for tonight," he said. "I'm going to bed."

"Fine," Stan replied, getting up from his folding chair. "I need to get another beer anyway." Retrieving a cloth hanging from the shelf, he placed it lovingly over his son's cherished invention. Turning back around, he was about to explain the importance of letting the machine cool off, but Danny was already gone.

14

THE TIRES

Still stinging from his father's rebuke the night before, Robert decided that morning to kill two birds with one stone: get a little payback on his dad while also adding another enhancement to his developing Action Bike.

The tiny tires on Robert's motorbike would be shredded like Frosted Mini-Wheats on Danger Peak's rugged terrain. He needed larger, sturdier tires to carry him up the mountain. Calling his two best friends before school began, he convinced them to come over to help him add larger tires to his vehicle, with the help of his dad's newly bought Toyota.

Fortunately, just before the summer, Robert's bike had been fitted with special wheels that resembled car wheels. It was a gift from his mother for graduating elementary school. He had won every award at his class's moving-up ceremony, except for "most improved."

Even then, Robert didn't like change. Of course, with his brother gone and his father uninterested, he had to do most of the work himself to customize his bike. His young back strained just from the memory of having to remove the fenders to fit the larger wheelbase.

From his front door, Robert watched as Chris's motorbike rode up the driveway and parked next to the garage. Chris was in the driver's seat with Rinnie seated behind him. Robert figured Rinnie's bike was still in the shop. After they entered the house, Robert led them quietly into the garage, hoping his parents, who were still upstairs getting ready for the day, wouldn't notice the commotion.

"I hope you know what you're doing," Chris groaned anxiously as he entered the garage with Rinnie right behind him. It was his habit to always bring up the rear.

"Yeah," Rinnie added, "what if your dad walks in?"

"He doesn't have to leave for work for another half hour."

Chris rubbed his temple worriedly. "That doesn't give us a lot of time."

"It'll be enough," Robert assured him.

"Just barely," Rinnie countered.

"Look!" Robert shouted, startling even them. "Do you want to spend the rest of the morning arguing, or do you want to get this over with?" Before his friends could respond, Robert handed Chris a lug wrench.

"Why do I have to remove the lug nuts?" he complained.

"Because I have to jack up the car," Robert explained, lifting up the heavy jack in his hand as evidence like they were five years old again in show and tell. Just thinking of kindergarten momentarily sparked a burst of warm nostalgia in Robert, and as he turned toward his dad's car, he caught a glimpse of the old recycling can that Danny and his father had used as a makeshift bench to work on the turbocharger. It had only been a few years ago, but it felt like eons. So much had happened in that time, it seemed like a different life.

"Uh, Rob?" Chris suddenly asked, snapping Robert out of his daydream. "Ya gonna jack up the car or what?"

"Oh, yeah, sorry," Robert apologized as he knelt near the front passenger's-side wheel and placed the jack underneath the car's frame. Then he began arduously pumping the jack as his father's Toyota slowly lifted off the oil-stained garage floor. "Oh, man," he admitted, his voice straining with effort at the task. "This is harder than I thought."

Feeling left out, Rinnie whined, "What am *I* supposed to do?"

"You have the most important job of all," Robert said a bit condescendingly. "You're our lookout."

"Lookout?" Rinnie asked, full of doubt.

"Yeah," Robert answered. "Stay by the garage door and look out for my mom."

Rinnie enthusiastically nodded. "Right," he said, practically saluting as he marched like an obedient soldier toward one of the large automatic doors at the front of the garage.

Robert stared at Rinnie, his mouth practically agape. "How were you never left back in school?" he asked.

Rinnie gave him a look like a puppy tilting his head to the side. "What?"

"Not *that* door!" Robert taunted. "The one that leads into the house! My mom's not going to be coming from *outside* the house!"

Rinnie corrected his position to stand guard at the proper door, all the while grousing, "Geez, man, I don't know the late-night habits of your mom."

Sensing an opening, Chris immediately pounced. "Yeah, but we know about *yours*," he said and then slapped Robert's hand in a spirited high five.

"That's so funny I forgot to laugh," Rinnie weakly retorted.

"Then why didn't you?" was Chris's typical reply.

"Alright, guys," Robert said, a serious tone creeping into his voice. "Enough horsing around. We have work to do."

At last, the car's front wheel was high enough for Chris to remove the lug nuts, and he swiftly unfastened them like a pro, so much so that Robert was awestruck. "How did you do that so fast?"

"Easy," Chris replied as he removed the tire and

placed it on the floor between them with a thud. "I just imagine that I'm in the pit crew of the Indy 500."

Robert smiled with ease, but his smile turned to a fearful grimace as Rinnie spoke up in a whispered warning. "Guys," he said, "I think I hear someone coming."

Everyone froze like they were playing the statue game, and the only sound in that garage was the panicked beating of Robert's heart. No matter what evasive maneuvers they took now, there was no hiding this.

After fifteen interminable seconds, Robert summoned the courage to ask Rinnie, "Who is it? Is it my mom?"

Rinnie pressed his ear against the door and then, after a beat, glibly shrugged. "False alarm," he announced sheepishly. "It was just the sound of the tire hitting the ground."

Robert and Chris both breathed a sigh of relief while simultaneously wanting to murder their friend for giving them a heart attack.

"Come on," Robert declared, snapping them out of their frozen fear, "one more wheel to go." In one fluid motion, Robert lowered the car, removed the jack, and then deftly maneuvered to the vehicle's back tire to place the jack in front of it.

Chris whistled in admiration. "And you were impressed with *me*?" he asked.

Robert laughed. "What can I say?" he asked as he

began pumping the vehicle off the ground again. "Your Indy 500 analogy inspired me."

Rinnie frowned. "If you guys can quit making out with each other for a minute, maybe we'll get out of here faster."

"Feeling left out again?" Chris mocked as he began quickly removing the lug nuts from the back tire.

"Wouldn't be the first time," Robert agreed.

"Har-har," Rinnie sarcastically mumbled to himself. Then his ears pricked up like a collie's. "Guys," he said, "someone's coming."

"Yeah, right," Chris said, unconvinced.

"No, seriously," Rinnie answered, "I mean it this time." The level of fear in his voice gave Robert some concern, and sure enough, just as Chris removed the second tire, the garage door attempted to open, with Rinnie slamming it back shut.

"Hey!" Robert's mom called from behind the door. "What's going on in there?"

Chris cursed and hid the tires behind the car as Robert instructed Rinnie to stall for time. As the garage door opened once more, Robert and Chris each took a position blocking one of the tires they removed, Robert shielding the front and Chris in back. Making sure his mom didn't see, Robert placed the lug wrench in his back pocket. Then Chris placed the lug nuts in his jeans pockets as Robert kicked the jack underneath the car.

"Oh, hey, Mrs. Kin!" Rinnie cheerfully greeted. "Didn't see you there."

"Hello, Rinnie," Donna answered wearily and with a whiff of impatience. "What're you boys doing in here?"

"Uh . . ." Rinnie was at a loss for words until Robert rescued him.

"We're just having another one of our Wild Boars meetings," he explained to his mom.

Donna knitted her eyebrows in confusion. "In our garage?" she asked. "And before school? Don't you boys normally have your meetings in your treehouse after school?"

"We, uh," Chris stammered, "wanted a change of pace today."

"Yeah," Rinnie added, somewhat clumsily, "variety is the spice of life." Robert gave him a look, telepathically conveying the message "Don't push it!"

"Anyway," Rinnie continued rudely, "we're almost done, so you can go now."

"What?" Donna asked, astonished and offended. "This is *my* garage, Rinnie."

"I just mean you can leave whenever you want is all," Rinnie said awkwardly.

Donna then peered over Rinnie's shoulder to call to her son. "Robert," she began, "I'm walking around the corner to get a breakfast bagel. Do you want one?"

"No thanks, Mom," he answered, still standing awkwardly to block his dad's missing tire.

She then noticed the portly Rinnie was nearly drooling at the mention of a breakfast bagel, and she reluctantly offered, "How about you, Rinnie?"

He was about to enthusiastically exclaim yes, but he could practically feel Robert's eyes boring into the back of his head in disapproval, so he changed his mind. "Better not," he said.

Donna's eyes squirmed in confusion at the odd reply. "Come again?" she asked.

"I mean 'no thank you,'" he quickly corrected himself as he attempted to suavely lean his arm against the wall to further obscure her view of her husband's prized, now two-wheeled car, but his hand accidentally landed on the garage door opener mounted to the wall. Automatically, the large bay door behind Stan's car began to open, and the two tires hiding in front rolled through the short gap and out of the garage.

"Oops!" Rinnie said as he clicked the button again to stop the door from lifting, but it was too late; the tires began rolling down the driveway. Luckily, Donna didn't seem to notice.

"Just be careful, boys, and don't be late for school," she suggested and then turned to leave.

As the door closed behind her, Robert ran after the tires. "Rinnie, I'm gonna kill you!" he shouted as he ducked under the partially open garage door to lunge for the runaway tires.

"Get in line," Chris added as he followed his club's leader.

Not seeing his mom in the driveway walking to the bagel store, Robert realized she must have exited their house from the side door in the kitchen since it was the one closest to the corner shops. It was a lucky break but small consolation as he desperately attempted to stop the tires.

Left alone in the garage, Rinnie suddenly felt self-conscious. He realized that if Robert's mom—or, worse, his dad—were to enter the garage now, he'd receive all the blame for their shenanigans.

"Hey, guys!" he called as he also ducked under the garage door. "Wait for me!"

15

CATCH THOSE TIRES!

The two large Goodyear tires slowly rolled down Robert's driveway. Even though they weren't moving very fast, they had a clear head start. As Robert and Chris frantically pursued them, they could see a truck turning the corner in front of the Kins' house.

"Great," Robert muttered as he pumped his young legs as quickly as he could. Gasping for air, he realized he wasn't going to make it in time before the tires collided into the oncoming traffic. The truck blew its ear-splitting horn as it attempted to swerve out of the way—even the driver knew there wasn't enough time to bring the long vehicle to a complete stop.

Never the athlete, Robert cursed himself for not having taken gym class more seriously as Chris passed him in a fevered sprint. Robert simply gave up and stopped to catch his breath. "Get them, Chris!" he called.

"What d'ya think I'm *tryin'* to do?" he answered, annoyed. With one last desperate move, Chris dove headfirst for the tires, his long arms outstretched in front of him. Amazingly, each hand grabbed each tire as they stopped at the foot of the driveway, with Chris's body slamming hard onto the asphalt and the truck passing within inches of the rubber rings. Crudely, the truck driver stuck a middle finger out of his window, aimed squarely at the boys, as he drove away.

"Thanks, man," Robert said as he approached his friend. "I owe you one."

"No," Chris disagreed, nodding toward the tires, "you owe me *two*."

"I guess you're right," Robert said as Rinnie finally joined them.

"I know I'm right," Chris said with confidence, "and you can start by lending me your hand." Robert lifted his friend off the ground, and Chris dusted himself off. Looking himself over, he noticed a small tear in the bottom corner of his *Miami Vice* T-shirt. "Aw, man," he complained, "this is my favorite shirt!"

Rinnie attempted to console him. "You can hardly notice it," he offered.

It didn't work. Suddenly, Chris turned on him in anger. "If it wasn't for you, I wouldn't have ripped it in the first place!" he argued.

"Hey, Chris," Robert said, trying to ease the

tension, "just feel lucky you're alive and that truck didn't squash your skull like a pumpkin." Chris had to concur that Robert was right. "Besides," Robert continued, snapping into club leader mode, "we're not out of the woods yet. Rinnie, go back inside and close the garage door and then meet us in my backyard."

"Why do *I* have to close the door?" he asked worriedly.

"Because you're the dumb one who opened it," Chris answered with force.

"Calm down," Robert instructed. "Let's go, Chris. You take one tire, and I'll take the other."

The three boys broke, two going through the gate that separated Robert's front and back yards and Rinnie reluctantly doing as he was told by crawling underneath the garage door's small gap that accidentally released the tires.

Robert opened the shed behind his house that stored his beloved dirt bike. The bike's old tires had already been removed before Chris and Rinnie arrived at the house. Robert knew there would be precious little time to make the switch that morning. "You still have the lug nuts, right?" he asked Chris.

"Yeah," he replied. "They're in my pockets."

"Good," Robert said. "We don't have much time before my dad goes to work. You put on the front tire, and I'll put on the back." The two went to work as Rinnie approached from behind.

"Hey, guys!" he called loudly as they both jumped.

"Geez, man!" Robert hollered as he tried fitting his dad's Toyota tire on his bike's frame. "Don't sneak up on us like that!"

"*You're* the one who told me to meet you guys here," Rinnie complained.

Chris saw red. "Rinnie," he began, "do you ever *not* whine?"

"Of course," he answered brightly, "I try to get ten hours of sleep a day."

Before Chris could reply with what was assuredly another smart-alecky comment, Robert called for attention. "We've got another problem, guys," he informed them. "The tires won't fit the bike. They're too large." Puzzled, Robert rubbed his chin. "I guess I should've seen this coming."

"Any ideas?" Chris asked.

"I've got nothing," Robert admitted.

"That's normally Rinnie's line," Chris noted, gesturing toward their younger friend.

"Hey, I'm full of good ideas," Rinnie protested.

"Okay, prove it, then," Chris taunted. "How can we get these tires on the bike?"

Instantly and without thinking, Rinnie replied, "Just let some of the air out."

Chris's rebuke was swift. "That's the dumbest—"

"Wait," Robert interrupted, removing the cap on his tire to let the air out, "that actually might work." As the air hissed out of the shrinking tube like a sighing snake, the Wild Boars watched the tire contract to a size that was compatible with the bike's enhanced frame, and Robert easily placed it on.

Chris stared in amazement. "I don't believe it," he said, his mouth agape.

"Told ya!" Rinnie rubbed it in his face, clearly pleased with himself.

"Okay," Chris admitted, "that's one for you. Now you only need about five thousand more to tie with me."

"Quick," Robert said, ignoring his friends' argument to focus on the task at hand. "Do the same with your tire as I screw in the nuts." Robert took the lug wrench from his back pocket and began screwing the nuts into the rear tire as Chris released some of the air from the front one.

Rinnie let out a small defeated sigh. "Let me guess," he began, "I'm on lookout again?"

"No need," Robert said proudly, tightening the last nut and then handing Chris the wrench. "We're almost done."

"I can't believe we're going to get away with this," Chris said as he replaced the cap on the tire and began screwing the nuts in. "What're you going to say when your dad finds out?" The question startled Robert, almost as if he had never thought of it before. Being his best friend, Chris seemed to sense this, asking, "You *do* have a plan, right?"

"I, uh," Robert began, hunting for the right words. "I'll think of something."

Disappointed, Chris shook his head. "You usually have a plan for everything," he said, losing faith in his so-called leader. Before Robert could respond, Chris placed the last lug nut in his tire and, in a bizarre demonstration, waved his hands like a morose magician and glumly stated, "Tah-dah."

For all the effort they had endured that morning, it seemed fairly anticlimactic, but Robert wasn't going to let Chris get him down. "C'mon, Chris," he said. "I'm going to test this baby. Hop on your bike and meet me at school."

Since the larger tires lifted his bike higher off the ground, Robert had to strain himself on his toes to properly mount it. He then revved his bike's engine to life as Chris walked toward the front of the house to retrieve his own bike.

"Wait for me," Rinnie said as he trailed Chris.

"You almost ruined this for us," Chris said, turning around in anger. "You can walk." And with that, Robert and Chris sped away in a cloud of smoke, leaving Rinnie literally in the dust to cough alone.

As the bikes turned down the end of the block to head for school, Rinnie heard Robert's father scream from the garage. "What the hell happened to my car?" he asked, and Rinnie didn't wait for him to repeat the question. He did as Chris instructed and ran to school as fast as his chubby legs could carry him.

16

BACK AT SCHOOL

During homeroom, without explanation, Robert and Chris were told they were reassigned a new technology teacher. Chris was about to ask why, but after sensing daggers in Robert's eyes, he thought better of it and let the subject drop. It was just as well, they figured. Now they wouldn't have to deal with Dr. Howard anymore.

Because Rinnie had to run to school, he was almost twenty minutes late. By the time he reached his first class, Spanish, he was given additional news. Besides being reassigned to another technology class, he was sent to the principal's office for being tardy. His teacher, Señora Martinez, explained this to him in Spanish, but not being the brightest student in class, Rinnie simply asked, "Qué?" After she translated her instructions into English, Rinnie, feeling dejected, walked out the classroom door, the laughter of his fellow students ringing in his ears.

On the way to the office, Rinnie realized that with all the commotion at Robert's house, he hadn't had time to eat breakfast that morning, so he stopped by the school's candy machine next to the teachers' lounge. As he carefully slid three quarters into the coin slot for a Snickers bar, he overheard Dr. Howard in the adjacent room.

"Oh, clumsy me, I slipped and fell in my bathroom," he said.

After grabbing the candy bar from the vending machine dispenser, greedily tearing off half the wrapper, and biting off a large chunk, Rinnie curiously peered into the teachers' lounge, being careful not to be seen. The white bandage was still wrapped around Dr. Howard's left cheek, but whenever his fellow teachers asked what had happened, he merely repeated the story he had told Robert's father: he had slipped and fell in his bathroom. Rinnie still wondered why he was covering for him and his friends. Could he possibly have a soft spot for them after all?

Dr. Howard then continued his story. "It's my latest—and greatest—invention," he proudly boasted to a semicircle of off-duty teachers. "I just completed it last night. I wasn't sure I'd have the final funds to pull it off, but let's just say something fell into my lap."

"Well, don't leave us in suspense, Forrest," Mr. Griffin, Rinnie's math teacher, asked. "What is it?"

"Yeah," Ms. Shore, an English teacher, sarcastically added, yawning as she did so, "we're on the edge of our seats."

Rinnie could see Dr. Howard smart a little, which made him think there might be some unrequited romantic history between the two of them, but he chased the thought away and concentrated on what his former technology teacher said next.

"It's a micro laser, small enough to fit in this pocket." He beamed, gesturing toward his oversized lab coat's front pocket. "But powerful enough to make an incision in that wall." Now he pointed toward the lounge door, where Rinnie was spying.

Quickly, Rinnie hid behind the vending machine before he could be identified. Suddenly, it seemed as if Mr. Griffin and Ms. Shore's roles had reversed.

"Sounds dangerous. Why would you even need such a thing?" Mr. Griffin asked skeptically, while Ms. Shore leaned in closer to Dr. Howard.

"Wow, just *how* powerful, Forrest?" she asked.

Leaning in himself to meet her body, Dr. Howard blushed but couldn't help himself. "It's *Doctor*," he corrected her. Ms. Shore frowned as Rinnie sped away back to class.

He knew this laser would be a breakthrough in his club's Action Bike project, and he couldn't wait to tell the others, but when he arrived at his Spanish class, Snickers bar in hand, his teacher stared at him, astonished.

"Rinnie," she scolded. "Qué pasa? You were

supposed to go to the principal's office, not the candy machine!" In all his excitement, he had forgotten the reason he left Spanish class in the first place.

Rinnie looked down at his candy bar and blanched a peculiar shade of crimson. "Oops," he said as the rest of the class laughed again in his direction.

"Vás!" she ordered, pointing toward the door as Rinnie turned around and headed back into the hallway.

The school bell rang, which meant now Rinnie was going to be late for his second class. As students filled the hallway, their gangly limbs knocked the candy bar out of Rinnie's hand. "Hey!" he shouted, annoyed. "My breakfast!" Clearly, this wasn't going to be one of Rinnie's better days.

On the other side of the school, Robert and Chris were busily talking about that morning's events while walking to their next class. It was like a secret joke they shared, and they knew the rest of the school probably wouldn't even believe them if they did share it. As they commiserated over Dr. Howard, they turned a corner and bumped into a tall teacher, knocking a stack of important-looking papers out of his hand. Embarrassed, Robert quickly bent down to retrieve them, not even bothering to see the person he had bumped into.

"Sorry, sir," he began, "we were just complaining about Dr.— " As he reared up to hand the teacher his papers, he realized he was talking to the man himself.

"Howard!" Chris finished his sentence in

astonishment. Even Rinnie's luck wasn't that bad, he thought.

"No!" Robert disagreed, sweating profusely like a flop comic bombing under hot lights. "We were talking about our dentists! You know, they're doctors too! Man, how we hate getting our teeth drilled."

"Spare me, boys," Dr. Howard said, raising a large commanding hand. "You're not fooling me. I realize you're not my greatest . . ." Struggling to find the proper word, he finally settled on "fans."

Chris pointed to the bandage on the teacher's cheek. "Sorry about your face, Dr. H.," he offered but secretly wanted to add, "It's quite an improvement." Dr. Howard softly caressed the white bandage on his cheek as if his hand possessed magic powers to heal it.

Finally, Robert summoned up the courage to plead for mercy. "Dr. Howard," he began, "I truly am sorry for what transpired the day before, and if you could find some way in your heart to forgive us and not publicize the news of the source of your impairment, we would greatly appreciate it."

Dr. Howard shook his head and chuckled, which was, to say the least, not the reaction Robert expected.

"Oh, Robert, true to form, you are entirely predictable," he began. "I can always tell when you're fibbing because of the number of four-dollar words you attempt to squeeze out of your usually limited vocabulary."

Not as bright as Robert, Chris was simply confused. "Huh?" he asked.

"He's saying he can tell I'm lying because I'm using big words," Robert helpfully explained.

"Oh," Chris blankly said.

"Nevertheless," Dr. Howard continued, "you two happen to be in luck. To be quite honest with you, the flypaper you so *creatively* used against me was a prototype, and I just secured a strict licensing agreement with the Blammo Company that if anyone should get hurt by my product, they're going to cancel my contract. It's a very lucrative deal, and this could be my ticket to an early retirement so I don't have to teach you bra—I mean *boys* anymore, so let's just keep this incident between us, okay?"

Robert didn't need any more convincing. "Deal!" he excitedly said, extending his hand to shake. Chris did the same, but Dr. Howard simply stared at their offering dismissively. Instead, he gave a half-hearted salute like the colonel he may have been in a past life.

"I'll be seeing you in the halls, boys," he said. "As I'm sure you're aware by now, you've been reassigned another technology teacher. The best thing for all of us, wouldn't you agree?"

"Yes," Robert replied—perhaps a little too quickly—as they parted ways.

"See you around," Chris called after the teacher as he was engulfed in the hallway by a throng of overexcited students and then faded away.

17

THE LASER

At lunchtime, Rinnie looked as if he were about to burst. "I'm so excited, guys!" he enthusiastically announced at the lunch table. "I can't wait to tell you what I found out. Hold on a second—" He then loudly cleared his throat and obnoxiously hooked a finger into his left nostril, prying a stalactite of snot loose. Chris stared at him, flabbergasted.

"What?" Rinnie innocently asked.

"Gross," Chris simply replied.

Robert was less subtle. "We're trying to eat here, Rinnie!" he yelled, throwing his homemade ham sandwich down in disgust on the aluminum foil.

"Oh yeah," Rinnie said, "sorry. But trust me. The info I have is worth it."

"It better be." Chris sighed.

"This morning," Rinnie began, "Señora Martinez

sent me to the principal's office for being late. Since I skipped breakfast, I stopped at the vending machine to grab a snack. At first, I was going to get something healthy like popcorn, but then I realized I hadn't had a candy bar in a while and decided to treat myself."

Chris started twirling his fingers in the air impatiently as if to say, "Get on with it," but Rinnie clearly didn't get the hint.

"So then I had to decide which candy bar to choose from. I was going to get a Milky Way, but the caramel sticks to my teeth. Then I realized I was in the mood for peanuts—"

"Rinnie!" Chris exploded, banging the table with his fist so hard that their milk cartons shook. "Get to the point before we die from boredom!"

"Oh yeah," Rinnie said. "Sorry. So, anyway, I ended up getting a Snickers bar, and then I heard Dr. Howard talking in the teachers' lounge next door. He said he just finished another one of his inventions with help from some extra funding or something."

Robert's eyes widened in realization. "He must be talking about the three hundred bucks my old man had to fork over last night," he explained. "What did he make?"

"A mini laser!" Rinnie replied. "He said it's small enough to fit in someone's pocket but can punch a hole through a wall."

Robert sloped back in his chair, impressed. "That's exactly what we would need to break up those boulders on Danger Peak."

"It is?" Rinnie asked. Then, after Robert and Chris shot him a telling look, he continued, "I mean, yeah, of *course* it is. I knew that. That's why I'm telling you guys."

Robert leaned into the table conspiratorially, deciding to hatch another plan. "We need to get that laser."

"You mean steal?" Chris asked. "Again?"

"I wouldn't technically call it stealing," Robert explained. "More like borrowing. We'll give it back to him once I return from Danger Peak."

"You mean *if* you return," Rinnie warned ominously, sending a shiver up their spines.

Robert shook it off. "It'll be fine," he said, dismissing Rinnie's statement before it sunk its teeth into his psyche.

Ever the pragmatic one, Chris asked, "Where are we going to find it?"

"I didn't see any lasers when I was in his closet," Robert began, acting like one of his favorite literary heroes, Encyclopedia Brown, "and there aren't any in the rest of his classroom. That only leaves one place: his home laboratory. We can look up his address in the phone book. Tonight, we go to work."

"I don't know, guys," Rinnie worried. "My bike's still in the shop, and I'm getting kinda tired of our adventures."

"Rin-*nie*," Chris said in a mocking tone of voice, "don't be a scaredy cat."

"I'm not!" Rinnie protested, but it was clear to his friends that was a lie.

Robert tried a gentler approach. "Rinnie," he began, "you really came through for us today, and we couldn't pull this off without you."

"Really?" he asked.

"Absolutely," Robert answered, smiling affectionately. "You did good, Rinnie."

"Yeah," Chris agreed, "it's a good thing I made you walk to school. Otherwise, you wouldn't have been late, been sent to the principal's office, and overheard that story."

"That's right," Rinnie proudly answered. Then, after contemplating what Chris just said, he added, "Wait—"

"You're finally getting the spirit of the Action Bike," Robert interjected.

"Thanks," Rinnie said. "Okay, I'll join you guys."

"Great," Robert said and took another satisfying bite out of his ham sandwich.

After a beat, Rinnie added, "Can I be leader now?"

Chris and Robert simply rolled their eyes.

18

MORE TROUBLE AT HOME

That afternoon, as soon as Robert returned home, he immediately grabbed the local phone book from the hallway closet and retreated upstairs to his bedroom to look up Dr. Howard's address. *That's right, Dr. Howard*, he thought. *You may have my home address on file at school, but I can also find yours.* As he flipped through the pages, he sang a little ditty in his head: "Let my fingers do the walkin', let my mouth do the talkin'." It was a commercial jingle for the Yellow and White Pages he had overheard on TV one day.

Once he landed on Howard's name, he was shocked—though delighted—to learn that the Wild Boars didn't have far to travel to infiltrate his home laboratory. He lived only twenty blocks away. With a man as strange as Dr. Howard, Robert had figured it was more likely he lived on Pluto than in his own hometown—and only a short ride away, no less. Robert quickly grabbed his novelty Garfield phone and called his friends to tell them to meet him at Dr. Howard's address in half an hour.

Robert raced downstairs to grab a quick bite to eat before he headed for his motorbike. Wanting to hurry out the door before his parents arrived, he still hadn't thought of a decent excuse about where his father's tires went, and he couldn't exactly explain that they magically disappeared. Since his father's car was no longer in the garage, Robert reasoned he must have gotten to work somehow. He knew his father was always prepared and most likely had more than one spare lying around.

Just as Robert was about to exit the house, he heard the garage door open. His father was home early.

⤶

On the other side of town, Chris had other problems to deal with. Namely, his own father. While he was trying to sneak out the backdoor to his dirt bike parked in the yard, his father had grabbed him from behind by the shoulder, making Chris jump half a foot in the air.

"Whoa!" Chris yelled.

"Sorry to scare you like that, champ," his father jovially said. "Where ya headed?"

"Uh, nowhere," Chris meekly responded.

His father sternly stared his son down. "'Nowhere' isn't a place I've ever heard of," he said. Then, mimicking a popular public service spot on TV, he added, "Chris, is your brain on drugs?"

"No!" Chris flatly denied, almost laughing at the absurdity of the question.

"Are you sneaking out to go on a date?"

"No!" Chris repeated.

"Because if you are, that'd be great!" his father answered, somewhat surprisingly. "It's about time you got out and mingled with the fairer sex."

Chris blanched and began rubbing his temple. "Dad," he began, humiliated, "please don't say 'fairer sex.'"

"Then what *are* you doing, Christopher?"

"I'm going to hang out with my friends, okay?" Chris finally answered.

"Who?" his Dad asked, clueless.

"Um, Robert and Rinnie?" Chris said in a "no duh" voice.

"Those guys?"

"Yeah," Chris answered sarcastically. "I've only been hanging out with them since kindergarten."

His father shook his head solemnly. "It's late, Christopher," he stated. "You can see them tomorrow."

"But *Daaaad*!" Chris whined. "Robert wants to show me the new modifications on his bike."

"Again, he can show you tomorrow," his father firmly ordered. "Now get ready for dinner. It's liverwurst supreme night."

Chris sighed, about to give in to defeat, when an

idea struck him. "Okay, you got me," he suddenly said. "I *am* going out on a date."

"You are?" his dad asked with excitement.

"Yes."

"What's her name?"

"Uh," Chris scanned his brain for a name and came up with Rinnie's crush. "It's Barbara."

"Pretty name," his dad complimented.

"I thought so too," Chris added.

"Guess we like the same type of women," his father proudly said. "You're a chip off the ol' block."

Chris began motioning toward the backdoor of the house again. "Thanks," he said, "I think."

"What does she look like?" his dad asked. "Like your mother?"

"Dad!" Chris shouted, his face flushing red. Before he had simply been embarrassed; now he was mortified.

"It's okay," his dad said. "You don't have to tell me."

"Great," Chris said, opening the rear door. "I'll let you know how it goes."

"Don't come back too late," his father called and then added with a mischievous chuckle, "and don't do anything I wouldn't do, heh-heh."

Chris simply rolled his eyes as he walked off into the fading sunlight.

Back at Robert's house, things weren't quite so sunny. Robert tried to hustle to his backyard shed to retrieve his dirt bike, but his father had other plans.

"Robert!" he called from the back porch. "Get in here now!" Robert slowly turned around to face the music. As he approached his house's rear exit, the intimidating shadow of his father filling the doorway, that music was a funeral hymn. Passing his father and entering the house, his face flinched, expecting a fresh slap, but, thankfully, none came. Luckily for Robert, Stan still had standards.

"Would you mind explaining to me what the hell happened to my tires?" he asked, doing his best to stifle his rage.

"What tires?" Robert asked. It was worth a shot.

"Oh, Robert," Stan began, "if you know what's best for you, you won't play dumb again."

"Are you talking about your car?" Robert asked.

"No," Stan sarcastically spat, "my toy train set downstairs. Of course my car!" For emphasis, he opened the adjacent garage door to reveal the two small spares on his Toyota, the lopsided car leaning comically like a drunken hobo. As Robert had suspected, his father was always prepared.

"I didn't take them," Robert protested, expecting either another verbal onslaught or an actual physical one.

Instead, his father simply lowered his eyes in disappointment. "I'm not going to waste any more of my time arguing with you," he said, his voice an ominous hush. "You're grounded for two weeks."

"What?" Robert asked.

"One week for each tire," Stan explained, slamming the garage door shut again.

"But that's not fair!" Robert complained.

"What's not fair is me being half an hour late to work because I had to replace my two missing tires," his father continued.

"I swear I didn't do it," Robert lied.

"Boy," Stan began with malice in his voice, "if you keep lying to me, I'm going to make it *three* weeks."

"He didn't do it," a soft voice wafted from the kitchen. Both Stan and Robert looked up to see Robert's mother. She had just come down from her bedroom upstairs. "The tires were gone this morning before he left for school. Someone broke into the garage overnight and took them. I was going to tell you as soon as you got home from work, but you didn't give me a chance."

Stan wasn't convinced. "If someone broke into the garage," he began suspiciously, "why wasn't there any broken glass this morning?" Robert's head sank to meet his chest.

"I fixed the glass before going for my morning breakfast bagel," Donna immediately answered as if she had rehearsed the line earlier.

"Since when did you become Mrs. Fix-It?" Stan asked his wife. "You need my help to change a light-bulb."

"Let's just say I've been quite bored this past year waiting for Robert to come home from school and you to come home from work, so I learned a few things on my own." She crossed her arms for emphasis.

Stan still wasn't entirely persuaded, but at this point, it was his wife's word against his common sense and better judgment. Despite getting to his job late, it had felt like a long day at work, and he didn't want to argue forever. At a loss for words, Stan simply stammered, "Well, that's . . . quite impressive then." Turning back toward his son, he looked as if he was going to issue an apology. Then, thinking better of it, he stormed off upstairs, muttering, "I'm gonna take a shower."

After making sure his father was out of earshot, Robert exhaled in relief. "Thanks, Mom."

"You're welcome, honey," she responded. Then, in a more serious tone, she added, "Listen, I don't know what you and your friends are up to, but this is the *last* time I'm going to bail you out. Okay?"

"Deal," Robert agreed, just ecstatic that he had gotten away with it this time. His mother winked, and Robert headed for the backyard.

"Don't come back too late," she called after him.

"I won't," he answered. But they both knew that was a lie.

19

THE LAB

The Wild Boars met at Dr. Howard's house, with Rinnie once again riding shotgun on Chris's dirt bike. It seemed Rinnie's own bike was stuck in purgatory at the repair shop. Since it was such a measly vehicle anyway, Chris thought they should just put it out of its misery.

As Robert and Chris turned off their motors and dismounted, they surveyed the smallish suburban home. It was modest but fairly standard for a teacher's salary, even one owned by a self-professed "star" of the school. Fortunately for them, it appeared the doctor was away. The windows were darkened in the one-floor house, and his car was absent from the driveway. Rinnie wondered if he had decided to take that teacher in the faculty lounge on a date. They were amazed that, for once, Dr. Howard seemed to have a life.

Cautiously, Robert and Chris walked their bikes around the house into the backyard as Rinnie crept close behind. When they entered the yard, they scanned the bottom half of the house, looking for a loose basement window they could pry open to enter the underground laboratory. Suddenly spotting one, Chris pointed and excitedly shouted, "Right there!"

"Shh," Robert shushed his eager friend. "Are you trying to blow our cover?"

"Yeah," Rinnie agreed in a hushed whisper, "that's why I brought this." He opened his backpack to retrieve a comically large fedora and fake mustache. Then he donned the oversized, floppy hat and squished the thin caterpillar of a mustache above his upper lip, sealed with Scotch tape.

Both Robert and Chris stared him down hard, but Chris was the first to speak. "Rinnie," he began, "what the hell is that?"

"It's my costume for Halloween," Rinnie explained. "It's a disguise so if we get caught, no one will recognize me."

"Rinnie," Robert started, "first of all, no one knows who you are."

"Yeah," Chris agreed, "and who are you supposed to be for Halloween anyway? A dork?"

"No, I was going as an older version of me," Rinnie answered.

"Exactly," Chris responded. "A dork."

"Take that stuff off," Robert ordered, ripping his mustache away like a stuck-on Band-Aid.

"Ow!" Rinnie yelped.

"*Shh*," Chris hushed. Robert then swiped Rinnie's hat and stuffed it in his coat pocket.

"Be careful with that," Rinnie warned. "It cost me five-fifty at Caldor."

"You were robbed," Chris said.

"Come on, guys," Robert said, motioning toward the window. "Anyone bring anything to jimmy this open?"

"I did," Chris replied, removing a crowbar from his backpack.

"Geez, you really *do* come prepared," Robert said, his eyes as wide as saucers.

"Where did ya even get that?" Rinnie asked, obviously impressed but trying to hide it out of pride.

"Swiped it from my old man's garage," Chris answered. "Where else?"

"Nice work, Chris," Robert said, smiling. Rinnie looked on enviously as Chris shimmied the hooked metallic bar into the slight space between the basement window frame and house. After using as much effort as his thirteen-year-old muscles could muster, he pried the frame loose and fully extended it so they could slip inside. The trio was about to loudly cheer when they remembered their surroundings and stealth cover.

"Okay," Rinnie quietly said, "who should go first?"

Robert and Chris looked at each other and then immediately turned back to Rinnie. "You should," they both said.

"Me?" Rinnie asked helplessly. "Why me?"

"Because this was your idea," Robert explained.

Rinnie was beside himself. "No, it wasn't," he protested. "It was yours."

"Yeah," Robert admitted, "but you were the one who overheard the story about Dr. Howard's laser."

"Why can't Chris go?" Rinnie asked, pointing to his taller friend.

"I brought the crowbar and opened the window," Chris said. "I already did my part."

Cornered, Rinnie sighed and shook his head. "Fine," he surrendered and hitched up his pant legs before squatting down so he was at eye level of the open window frame.

Chris cocked his head to the side and squinted, sizing up the difference between Rinnie's portly body and the small window. "It's gonna be a tight fit," he announced.

"I know," Rinnie agreed. "This is why you guys should go."

"We're all going in, or none of us are," Robert ordered. "It's all for one and one for all, remember?"

"That's the Three Musketeers," Chris said. "We're the Wild Boars."

"Yeah," Rinnie added. "Our motto is supposed to be 'just have fun.' And I gotta say, I'm not having much fun right now."

"Rinnie," Robert continued, the anger seething in his voice, "just go in there before I shove you in myself!"

"Fine," Rinnie glumly answered and lowered his

body flat to the cold, wet ground, "but you guys owe me another one for this."

Robert and Chris simply smiled in amusement as Rinnie squeezed the first half of his body through but got caught around the midsection.

"Look," Chris said to Robert, nodding a thumb toward Rinnie's wiggling rear, "it's Rinnie the Pooh."

"Ha-ha, guys," Rinnie's voice faintly mumbled from behind the pane of glass.

"Let me help ya, Rin," Chris said and swiftly kicked him in the behind.

"Hey!" Rinnie yelped as he tumbled forward onto the basement floor with a resounding thud.

"That wasn't very nice," Robert told Chris.

"No," Chris agreed, "but it was fun."

"Come on," Robert said, "you're next."

Always faithful to his leader, Chris lowered himself and slid through the tiny basement window.

"Thanks, Rinnie," Chris said as he softly touched down into the basement. "I think you made the hole bigger."

"Shut up, Chris!" Rinnie yelled and then began striking Chris's shoulders with small, weak blows.

"Quit it, man!" Chris yelled back as he grappled with Rinnie's arms and almost knocked an adjacent shelf of knickknacks over in the scuffle.

Robert quickly bounded into the basement to break up the fight. "Knock it off, guys!" he ordered. "You're going to break Dr. Howard's stuff."

"Who cares?" Chris asked, still wrestling with Rinnie against the wall.

"We're here to steal things, not break them," Robert argued with an air of superiority.

"Such a great moral code, dear leader," Chris responded, the dry sarcasm surprising even him.

"Tell him to stop picking on me!" Rinnie pleaded with Robert, struggling to maintain his balance in the scuffle.

"You're the one who wants to play *Rocky*!" Chris countered.

"Stop it, both of you!" Robert ordered once more, physically inserting himself between his friends. "We've got bigger things to worry about. We have to find the laser before Dr. Howard gets home, which could be any minute."

Chris and Rinnie finally stopped tussling and turned away from each other, arms crossed like a pair of mismatched roommates in a cheesy, laugh-track-heavy sitcom.

"I'm not helping until Chris apologizes," Rinnie said stubbornly.

"Then you're going to be waiting until the new millennium," Chris warned.

"Fine," Robert said, retrieving a flashlight from his backpack and flicking it on. "Screw both you guys, then." He stalked off, swerving the beam of his light to and fro to search for the elusive laser. Slashing at the darkness with his flashlight, he was briefly reminded of the days he had played with toy lightsabers in his back-yard with Danny.

"Hey, wait up," Rinnie and Chris both said. Realizing they uttered the exact same words, they turned to each other and gave a half-smile.

"Jinx," they said, and it was as close to an apology as either was going to get.

After Rinnie and Chris caught up with Robert, the three boys scanned the assorted shelves looking for anything remotely laser-like. To their curious young eyes, they discovered reams of wire bunched in coils like Slinkys, broken cardboard boxes of miscellaneous nuts and bolts, half-finished robotic skeletons, and other metallic junk—but no laser. In many ways, Dr. Howard's basement lab was just an oversized extension of his classroom closet back at school.

Even though it was clear Dr. Howard wasn't home yet, the three kept their silence like altar boys in church. They reasoned they had quarreled enough that late afternoon and didn't want to push their luck. As they perused the various objects scattered about two work-benches and four trays of beakers, the quiet was almost reverential until, at last, Rinnie broke the silence.

"I think I found it," he announced in a subdued tone that didn't sound like his normal cheerful self.

"How can you tell?" Chris asked.

Rinnie pointed to a sign in the corner of the basement. "Because the sign says, 'New laser prototype,'" Rinnie helpfully explained.

Feeling dumb, Chris swallowed his pride and followed Rinnie and Robert to the corner of the room. Indeed, the sign didn't lie. There it was: a small, curved, silver tube mounted to a plastic cartridge filled with intricate microchips. In food terms, it mostly resembled a large piece of elbow macaroni attached to a box the size and shape of a graham cracker.

Robert was hesitant to pick it up. Not only was he cautious that he might accidentally trigger it, but the whole scenario felt like a trap to him. Why would Dr. Howard label his own creation when nothing else in the basement was labeled? Was he wise to the three boys after they swiped his—or, rather, Danny's—turbocharger? Also, it seemed awfully convenient that the rear basement window had been slightly ajar.

"Well," Chris told Robert, "what are you waiting for? Pick it up."

Robert gingerly lifted the tiny contraption like Indiana Jones removing the idol from the temple in the opening scene of *Raiders of the Lost Ark*. He finally decided to divulge what was on his mind.

"Guys, I don't like this," he said as he scrutinized the prototype, turning it over in his hands like a jeweler inspecting a newly arrived precious stone. "This was all too easy."

"Easy?" Rinnie asked, flabbergasted. "You call falling onto the basement floor and almost killing myself and then Chris and I almost killing each other *easy*?"

"Quiet, Rinnie," Chris warned and then pitched

his head up toward the house's first floor. "I think I heard something."

"It feels like a trap," Robert explained. "Why would Dr. Howard label this laser when nothing else was? Maybe he's on to us."

Suddenly, the basement door opened, and the light flicked on. Then Dr. Howard began descending the flight of stairs with Ms. Shore, the teacher from the faculty lounge.

"Here," he began, proudly gesturing his hand toward the weird gadgets and gizmos strewn across the floor, "let me show you my latest prototype."

"Or maybe he was just trying to impress his date," Rinnie whispered as the three boys hauled toward the open window.

Halfway down the stairs, Ms. Shore unexpectedly announced, "It's chilly down here," and as if to prove it, she wrapped her arms around herself for warmth.

"Let me help you," Dr. Howard said, leaning in closer to place his arm around her midriff.

"That's okay," Ms. Shore said as she abruptly nudged him aside. Dr. Howard seemed to grimace from the perceived slight. "Looks like you left your window open," she continued, pointing to the agape half-window.

"What?" he asked and quickly shuffled his middle-aged legs down the stairs. Before he could reach it, Robert and Chris hoisted Rinnie through the window. Then Robert lifted Chris after him as Dr. Howard shouted, "You again!"

Robert didn't dare turn around as, with his back toward the teacher, he hid the laser inside Rinnie's novelty hat. Dr. Howard reached out for Robert just as Rinnie and Chris grabbed him from above and pulled him through the window.

"Let's get out of here!" Rinnie exclaimed as Robert and Chris were already mounting their bikes and revving the engines to life. Chris shook his head at how pointless Rinnie's direction was, but given the circumstance, he decided to let it go.

Inside the basement, Ms. Shore asked, "Who were they? Students of yours?"

"Intruders," Dr. Howard simply answered with venom in his voice. He then grabbed his basement phone to dial 9-1-1. This time, he wasn't calling school security.

20

THE WOODS

As Robert and Chris sped away from Dr. Howard's house, with Rinnie sitting behind Chris and holding on for dear life, the three friends celebrated with a triumphant cheer, but their victory was short-lived. Seconds after turning down the end of their former instructor's block, they heard a pair of sirens in the air. Robert swallowed hard. It was clear those sirens were not only real, but they were meant for them.

"What, does Dr. Howard have the police on speed dial?" Rinnie asked.

"It's the cops, lame brain," Chris shot back through the gusts of air lapping their faces. "He doesn't need speed dial. He just has to call 9-1-1!" The Wild Boars couldn't yet see their pursuers, but that didn't stop them from formulating a plan. As ever, Chris turned to his leader. "What do we do, boss?" he asked. "Evasive action time again?"

Robert thought for a frenzied moment and then shook his head. "No need to split up," he explained. "They can't chase us in the woods." As Robert banked left onto Pine Street, Chris followed closely behind—a little too close, in fact. Finally revealing itself, a cop car screeched around the corner behind them. Distracted by the noise, Chris turned his head to glance behind him and almost rammed into Robert's back tire.

"Look out!" Rinnie warned, pointing ahead. Chris instinctively whipped his head back toward the front and clutched the brakes on his handlebars, his front tire missing Robert's vehicle by inches.

"Watch it!" Robert scolded as they headed toward the greenery of the town's forest.

"Sorry," Chris apologized as he sped alongside Robert so they weren't lined up in a collision course.

"Remember," Rinnie reminded Chris, "if you wipe out, *I* wipe out."

"Don't tempt me," Chris rejoined.

"Save it for later," Robert recommended as a second cop car whizzed by their right side. "Looks like the boys are back in town."

Given the dire circumstances they found themselves in, Chris attempted to lighten the mood by mock-singing Tiffany's hit song. "Don't think we're alone now," he warbled, slightly changing the chorus.

With one cop car behind them and one flanking

their side, they were practically surrounded, and the driver behind them noted as much with his bullhorn.

"Pull over, boys!" he advised. "Let's talk this out!"

"Nothin' doin'," Robert muttered to himself as he accelerated his dirt bike to and through the forest perimeter, with Chris matching his stride. Both Robert and Chris easily trampled over the low brush lining the entrance but then had to quickly maneuver around the fast-approaching thicket of trees, almost colliding with each other in the process.

"Give me room!" Chris ordered.

"You're the one who almost crashed into me before," Robert reminded him.

As Rinnie dug his sausage-like fingers into Chris's stomach, fearful tears lining his cheeks as tiny rivulets, he whined, "Let's just get through this safely, okay, guys?"

Both Chris and Robert answered by taking separate paths. "Guess we have to split up again after all," Robert admitted.

"See you on the other side!" Chris called out to Robert, but he was already gone, lost in the lush brush of the densely packed forest. Chris tried to spot him, but Robert's green bike was easily camouflaged by the leaves, an extra benefit for evading the police.

As dozens of trees whizzed by Robert's bike, the sides of his legs almost glancing the bark, he thought about the exciting speeder bike chase sequence from the movie *Return of the Jedi*. Simply recalling *Star*

Wars conjured memories of seeing the movie repeatedly on VHS in Danny's bedroom and then reenacting the scenes with his brother using the iconic Kenner toys. As the warm, wistful memories swirled in his subconscious, Robert was whipped back to reality when a low-hanging tree branch practically knocked him off his bike. He knew he might not be as lucky next time, and daydreaming in his subconscious could lead him to being unconscious . . . permanently.

As he progressed further into the woods, the forest was becoming denser, the spaces between the trees narrowing. Just then, Robert got an idea. He dug into the floppy novelty hat Rinnie had brought along to their "heist" and retrieved the small silver laser tube. Quickly hooking it into a power source on the bike's front while still attempting to maintain control of his vehicle, Robert aimed the laser's barrel at the closest tree and pressed down on the power button built into the side of the invention. Instantly, a red blast of energy projected out of the tube's circular opening, slicing the tree in half. *Crack!* The two halves of the trunk fell on opposite sides of each other, and Robert easily drove right through the center, bouncing over the stump.

The smoldering embers smelled of scorched earth as Robert passed through the burnt bark, its seared edges still flickering an orangey yellow flame. In a brief, absurd moment, he felt like a circus lion leaping through a ring of fire.

"Good job, Dr. Howard," Robert said to himself with a wry smile.

Robert blasted several other trees in his way until he felt like he was playing a Nintendo game. Each easily fell to construct a unique obstacle course that he had to navigate through. The larger tires of his father's car rolled comfortably over the smaller fallen logs on the forest floor, and in the back of his mind, Robert wondered how his improved bike would handle the hazards of Danger Peak, which loomed ominously in the distance. But again, there wasn't much time for contemplation—only concentration on his expert riding skills, lest he topple over the bumpy forest debris.

A giant tree with an enormous base, possibly the widest in the entire forest, was quickly advancing. Robert deftly maneuvered his bike around the massive tree stump, and as he zoomed past the knotty base, he could see its twisted roots lining the soil like intricate natural calligraphy.

Robert's dirt bike bounced precariously up and down over the many tree roots, rocks, and sand mounds, and just when he thought the vibration would shake his vehicle apart, he spotted a clearing up ahead. It looked like the remains of a previous forest fire. Immediately, Robert steered his bike into the open area, relieved that he was more than halfway through the woods to meet Chris and Rinnie on the other side. Robert smiled with relief when, suddenly, a squirrel leaped from a tree onto the ground directly in front of him.

Robert forcefully swerved his bike to the left and almost smashed into a tree. The swift jerky motion caused him to lose balance, and he fell off his bike, rolling several times into the base of a large tree. Robert watched his bike skid to a halt near some thick brush. Luckily, there appeared to be minimal damage, and the engine was still purring.

In a rush to mount his bike once more, Robert leaped to his feet, only to feel a sharp sting jabbing his left ankle. He yelped in pain as he realized it was sprained. To add insult to injury, at that moment, the squirrel he weaved around to avoid came prancing past him.

"Thanks, man," he said sarcastically to the capering animal, which, in his mind, seemed to be comically chittering away at Robert's spill.

Robert looked behind him, and it seemed the coast was clear. The cop cars obviously couldn't follow him into the dense forest. His plan had worked. Now he just had to escape the woods before nightfall. Fortunately, he wasn't too far from the edge, where his suburban town gave way to more navigable sidewalks and streets again.

Wincing in pain, Robert hobbled toward his bike, carefully lifted it so the seat was aligned with his waist, and gently hopped on. Revving the engine a few times to make sure it was still operational, he then squeezed the accelerator and took off, a little slow at first to regain his balance and then almost at full speed. Since he knew he was no longer being chased, he kept his speed far below the maximum limit.

After a few minutes of carefully navigating the maze

of the woods, he saw an exit up ahead. Robert's ankle was still throbbing, and he couldn't wait to get home. He sped further toward the forest's opening, delighted that he had completed his journey—and mostly intact. The only lingering question was whether Chris and Rinnie had made it as well, but when he finally exited the forest, he realized he had nothing to fear; Chris and Rinnie were sitting on Chris's bike, patiently waiting on the other side.

"Slow poke," Chris teased his friend with a half-smile.

"Yeah," Rinnie added, "what took you so long?"

"I had some trouble, but I'm okay now," Robert explained. "Let's go."

"You don't have to tell me twice," Chris said excitedly as he revved his bike into high gear. Just as they were about to turn around and go home, a pair of cop cars sped to a stop on either side of them to block their path.

Chris lowered his head. "And you thought this was going to be easy," he said.

21

THE COPS

A tall, burly police officer with a mustache that rivaled Tom Selleck's on *Magnum P.I.* stepped out of the cruiser closest to Robert. "It's over, boys," he said gravely. "Dr. Howard said if you return the part you stole, he won't file charges."

"Never!" Chris shouted in an immature tone. Robert whipped his head toward Chris, surprised by the outburst. "Right?" he asked his club's leader.

"There's nothing we can do, Chris," Robert admitted. "We're surrounded. They've won." Still smarting from his sprained ankle, Robert gingerly set his bike's kickstand in place and dismounted. Then he slowly opened the secret compartment in the back of his bike and retrieved a long, silvery piece of metal. Finally, he stepped over to the officer and handed him the contraption. "Here," he said, defeated.

"Thanks, son," he said while placing the trinket in his back pocket. "Now let's get you boys home. We'll be following close behind, so no tricks this time."

Chris shot a daring look at Robert as if to say, "C'mon, we can make a break for it!" Having been on the same wavelength since kindergarten, Robert practically read his mind. For a moment, Chris was ready to sprint away, but instead, Robert dashed his hopes.

"It's no use," he said somberly as he returned to his bike to release the kickstand. "They already have the laser." After hopping on, Robert made sure the officer was back behind the wheel with the door closed before leaning in to furtively add, "It's just not the *real* one."

"Huh?" Chris asked. Robert slyly flashed the contents of the inside of Rinnie's floppy hat: it was Dr. Howard's laser from the lab.

Thoroughly confused, Chris asked, "Then what did you just give—"

Before he could finish, Robert explained as the two pairs of bikes and cop cars began slowly traveling toward Robert's home several blocks away. "I knew we might get into a jam like this, so I created a decoy," he said. "I swiped a piece of copper pipe from my dad's toolbox."

"Mint!" Chris said.

"Awesome!" Rinnie squealed in turn.

"Well, I can't take all the credit," Robert confessed with as much modesty as he could muster. "I got the idea from an episode of *MacGyver.*"

"I knew there was a good reason to watch that show," Chris cracked.

Just then, Robert's foot accidentally slipped off his bike's footrest, and he barked in pain. Rinnie's puppy-dog eyebrows rose in sympathy. "What's the matter?" he asked.

"I sprained my ankle in the forest after getting thrown off my bike by a squirrel," Robert explained.

"A squirrel?" Chris asked skeptically, leaning in for another turn down the block.

"Never mind," Robert said. "It's why I was late. Anyway, I have bigger problems now."

"What's that?" Rinnie asked.

"Facing my father," Robert said.

When the four vehicles arrived at Robert's house, Chris and Rinnie wished him luck before being escorted away again by the cops toward their respective homes. Robert wondered what fate awaited his friends. After all, their parents weren't much more understanding than his. But that was their problem now.

After stashing his bike in his family's backyard shed, Robert swallowed a deep breath of crisp night air before hobbling over to his home's rear entrance. Worryingly, the patio light ignited before he even reached the door. There, standing in the doorframe, was the hulking shadow of his father. This wasn't going to be easy.

As a mock "courtesy," Stan opened the backdoor for Robert and gruffly ordered, "Get in." As Robert stepped inside, head bowed low, he felt like he was six years old again, getting caught stealing an Oreo from the kitchen pantry. Absently, he wondered if he should bend over as his dad removed his belt to spank him.

A miniature laser worth thousands of dollars was a far cry from an Oreo. It was even a far cry from a turbocharger. He knew a simple spanking wasn't nearly a high enough price. "Sit down," Stan continued his orders, pointing to a kitchen chair. Robert carefully seated himself, still favoring his swollen ankle and wondering where his mother was. He suddenly realized that she wasn't kidding when she had told him she could no longer protect him. Robert was utterly alone.

"What were those cops doing outside our house?" his father asked. "Just what in the hell are you and your friends up to?"

Robert paused to compose himself, as if by stalling long enough he could come up with the perfect answer, no matter how futile that idea sounded. But his dad only allowed a few seconds.

"Answer me, Robert!" he demanded angrily.

"Fine," Robert said, all out of excuses at that point. "Chris, Rinnie, and I broke into Dr. Howard's lab—"

"You *what*?" Stan asked, astonished.

"W-we entered his basement laboratory," Robert stammered, substituting the euphemism *entered* for *broke into*, but his father wasn't fooled. "We stole, uh, *borrowed* a laser device he invented the other day."

Stan crossed his trunk-like arms across the wide barrel of his chest, and Robert briefly flashbacked to all the fallen logs his bike had ridden over earlier that afternoon.

"Why in the world did you do that?" Stan asked.

Robert switched course and made a weak attempt at humor, referencing a popular song that he had overheard his father singing in the car one day. "Don't worry, Dad," Robert said. "Be happy!"

Stan stared him down with a pinpoint focus, as if the laser that Robert snatched from Dr. Howard's lab was now powering his pupils. Robert sighed as he realized his father wasn't buying it.

"Don't tell me another lie like you sold it or lost it!"

"No, I didn't sell or lose it," Robert said. "I gave it back to the police."

Now Stan began angrily pacing back and forth in front of his son like a warden guarding his prisoner. "Boy," he began, "if I find out you're lying—"

"No, honest, Dad," Robert interrupted. "You can call the police if you don't believe me."

"I just might do that," Stan said, grabbing Robert's leg.

"Ow!" Robert squealed as he further twisted his sprained ankle.

"Come now," Stan said in a more measured tone of voice, "I didn't grab you that hard."

"No, it's not that," Robert said. "I sprained my ankle today."

Suddenly, a feminine voice cried out in alarm by the stairs. "What happened?" Robert's mother came rushing into the kitchen from the hallway, and it was at that moment he realized he wasn't alone after all. She had been listening to the conversation the entire time.

"I sprained my ankle when I fell off my bike," he repeated.

"Oh, you poor thing," his mother replied, her supportive voice oozing an overdose of empathy in an attempt to cover up the lack from her husband. "I'll go fetch some bandages." As she retreated to the nearest bathroom, Stan was relentless.

"I told you that bike of his was dangerous!" he called to his wife, who was fiddling in the cabinet beneath the sink. She then returned with an Ace bandage.

"Which ankle is it, sweetie?" she asked, kneeling to the floor. Robert pointed to his left ankle, and after he removed his sneaker and lifted the lower cuff of his jeans, his mother began lovingly wrapping the bandage around his foot.

"You come from good genes, Robert," his father suddenly said as if continuing an inner monologue no one else had been privy to. "How could you be so stupid?"

"Stan!" his wife scolded, turning her face toward him while still wrapping her son's ankle in the gauzy material. "Have a heart. He sprained his ankle today."

"I don't care if he sprained his *brain*," he replied.

Then, pivoting to his son, he gave his verdict: "You're grounded for an entire month."

"But, Dad—" Robert whined.

"I don't want to hear it!" his father bellowed. "That's it! End of story." He then barged off upstairs to retreat to his bedroom. It was getting late, and he had to get up early for work the next day.

After a moment of silence, as if to let what had just transpired sink in, Robert's mother lifted her head to speak. "Your father means well," she tried explaining, "and he *does* love you. He just has a funny way of showing it sometimes."

"Yeah," Robert said, "*really* funny. I wish I was laughing."

Choosing not to respond, as she knew it was an argument she wouldn't win, his mother finished tightening the bandage on Robert's ankle and stood up.

"There," she said, softly patting his wounded leg. "Right as rain."

"Thanks, Mom," Robert said.

"Of course," she said, smiling with affection. "Now go upstairs to wash up. I'll tell the school tomorrow you need a day of rest. Maybe I'll take you to Dr. Jacobs."

"Okay," he said and slowly got up from his chair.

After climbing the stairs, one careful step at a time, Robert passed his parents' bedroom as he walked toward the master bathroom. With the door half open, he caught a glimpse of his father getting ready for bed. They locked eyes for a moment, and then Robert continued hobbling away. Before he reached the bathroom, his father called out, a bit guilt-stricken, "Do you need any help?"

"That's okay," Robert replied. "I can manage."

"Alright," his dad said. He was about to say more when Robert closed the bathroom door behind him.

22

FINAL FLASHBACK

Robert was blissfully blasting his proton pack at a slimy, supernatural specter in New York's Penn Station alongside Peter Venkman when he was suddenly shaken out of his dream. Rapidly blinking his eyes, he awoke to find his brother, Danny, sitting on the edge of his bed and lightly nudging him awake. He was wearing the typical wardrobe emblematic of teenage rebellion: ripped blue jeans and a black T-shirt.

"Hey, Rob," he greeted softly.

Robert looked like he saw a ghost—and not the one in his dream. "Danny?" he asked in a craggy voice. After rubbing the crust out of his eyes, he turned to his He-Man alarm clock. The molded figurine bust was brandishing a sword with a built-in LCD display on the hilt, indicating that it was only a little past five in the morning. Fearing the worst, his heart began to race. "What's going on? Is everything okay?"

"Yeah, everything's fine," Danny reassured his younger brother. "You looked like you were having a pretty intense dream."

Robert sat up in his bright-orange X-wing fighter pajamas. "I was. I was dreaming I was a Ghostbuster."

Danny mildly chuckled so as not to wake their parents, who were still sleeping in their bedroom next door. Pointing to Robert's PJs, he noted, "I thought you were dreaming of being Luke Skywalker again."

Robert looked down and smiled. "Nah," he said. "We haven't played *Star Wars* in a while, so it hasn't really been on my mind."

"Just on your clothes," Danny quipped.

"I guess," Robert said, yawning. "Danny, why'd you wake me up so early? I don't have to get up for school for another two hours."

Danny paused for dramatic emphasis and then finally revealed his reason for the early wakeup call. "Robby," he began, "I'm going to climb Danger Peak."

Robert's eyes lit up like a pinball machine in the dark room. "You are?"

"Yep." Danny proudly beamed.

"That's awesome!" Robert shouted, lunging forward to hug his brother, but Danny gently held him back, putting a finger to his lips.

"Shh," he warned. "Don't wake up Mom and Dad."

"Why not?" Robert asked.

"Well," Danny began, "they're not exactly thrilled with the idea. Danger Peak is no bunny slope. Why did you think I was waking you up so early?"

"I dunno," Robert slurred, still half asleep. "You were too excited and couldn't wait for me to wake up to tell me the news?" Danny didn't answer. He only glanced at the nightstand clock impatiently as if he couldn't wait to get out of there to climb that mountain. Always hating awkward silences in conversations, even at that young age, Robert blurted out, "I'm real proud of you, Danny," as if he were their father, which spurred its own awkward moment.

Danny lifted his biker helmet, which until then had been partly obscured by the other side of the bed, and laid it in his lap. Then he lovingly placed it on top of his brother's smaller head. The larger helmet comically wobbled to and fro, and for a moment, Robert looked like a little boy playing with his parents' oversized clothes.

"Who knows?" Danny asked. "Maybe one day you'll make *me* proud and take on Danger Peak yourself." Robert smiled and held the helmet in place with one hand. "Alright, kid," Danny said while removing the helmet. "I'll see you around."

Danny got up from the bed and headed for the door, but before he could open it, Robert called out to him. "Danny?"

"Yeah?" he asked, turning around, his hand still on the doorknob.

Robert swallowed hard, afraid to ask the next question. Then, biting his lower lip, he summoned the courage. "What if you don't make it back?"

Danny simply flashed that famous smile of his. "Hey," he said, "anything worth doing is worth doing once."

It was a Thursday morning. Robert sat alone at his kitchen table in a dark sport jacket and black slacks, waiting for his parents to arrive. All he could do was stare blankly at the blue wallpaper. He tried not to dwell on the reason for his wait, so he concentrated on insignificant matters like buying a 7-11 Slurpee later on.

Robert rose from the table to painstakingly count sixty-five cents of spare change from the dome-shaped ceramic container on the soiled counter with his pointer digit. In that kitchen, he realized that he wasn't just alone for the moment but would be alone for an extended period of time afterward—perhaps a lifetime.

Just then he heard a familiar automobile horn softly being tapped outside his house. Robert left through his front door, turned around to lock it, and carefully stepped into the backseat of his mom's brown Pontiac station wagon parked in the driveway. Forcing a half-baked smile, he gave his parents a nod of encouragement. His father was in the driver's seat, and his mother sat beside him, massaging his arm.

After a wordless drive to the building, Robert

wandered inside while pondering which flavor Slurpee to purchase. He then climbed a nearby set of stairs and entered the packed room. It seemed everyone in the rows of seats was boring their eyes into the base of his skull. His mother held his twelve-year-old hand as he curiously approached the coffin at the funeral. Then, after releasing his mother's hand, he silently said good-bye to his brother lying within the casket.

Cherry, he thought. *I'll get a cherry Slurpee.*

23

DETERMINED

Robert didn't get much sleep that night. He stared at the ALF, Garfield, and Muppets posters on his walls and wondered why they were still there. It was like he was suspended in animation at eight years old, but that was five long years ago. Too much had happened, yet not enough within him had changed. He was still obsessed with his past, still stuck with the same feelings, and, most of all, still thinking about Danny. Sometimes he feared he wasn't truly honoring his brother with memories of him but, rather, his memories of his memories until, like a faded photograph, his brother's true identity would simply disappear over time.

Robert thought about the final night he saw Danny. He had dreamed about being a Ghostbuster and was wearing *Star Wars* pajamas. They weren't much different from the childish signifiers adorning his room. Robert wondered if he was going to stay stuck being a kid forever—embalmed in preadolescence for eternity like some museum curio.

Just then, a shaft of light pierced one of the slats in his window shutters, illuminating a small corner of the room where his helmet lay. The sun was starting to rise, and Robert thought if this wasn't a sign, he didn't know what would be. He also thought about America and the American dream. Mounting Danger Peak was *his* dream, and as the patriotic song "America the Beautiful" swelled in his mind, he realized he couldn't quit now. He had come too far. He had to do it. For his club. For his town. For Danny. And, if nothing else, for the "mondo cash" that Rinnie was always crowing about. Most importantly, he had to conquer the mountain that had conquered his brother.

Robert again looked at his bike helmet in the corner, now fully aglow in the sunlight with an almost supernatural luminescence. He then turned to gaze at his desk drawer, where his walkie-talkie hid inside. Robert gritted his teeth. It was time. Immediately, he changed out of his sweatpants into a long-sleeved *Robotech* shirt and blue jeans. He then strapped on his safety helmet and placed the walkie-talkie in his back pocket. Next, he opened his bedroom window that faced the backyard. Normally, he would wear a coat, but he didn't want to risk waking his parents by creeping downstairs to retrieve it.

Using his house's drainpipe like a fireman's pole,

he slid down slowly onto the soft grass below. Finally, he shuffled his Reeboks across the lawn to his shed and then opened it to reveal his prized possession: the Action Bike.

Though he was still supposed to be sleeping, Rinnie had set his alarm early so he could try beating his high score before school on a course he created in the 8-bit Nintendo game "Excitebike." Keeping the volume low on his large, boxy TV set, and hiding himself underneath the covers in his bed, his thumbs frantically pressed the A and B buttons and sleek cross-pad on the rectangular black-and-gray controller. Similar to a bowler performing a good-luck dance after rolling the ball down the lane, he even twisted his arms in wildly exaggerated movements, hoping this would improve his game. Just as his tiny motocross man on the screen was about to scale the giant pyramid he had constructed on the course, there was a knock on his door.

"Rinnie, go back to sleep!" his mother called. "You have to get up for school in less than an hour."

Rinnie rolled his eyes, wondering if his mom possessed the hearing of Superman. "Oh, Mom," he whined, "do I have to?"

His mom suddenly chose to go to DEFCON 1. "Turn the game off now, or I'll wake your father and have him do it for you!" Rinnie's mom knew how frightened he was of his old man, even more so than of Vinny and the other bullies at school. Nothing more needed to be said.

"Okay, okay!" Rinnie surrendered and got up to switch off his game and TV. "I'll never get past this course," he muttered bitterly under his breath. But instead of going directly to bed, he retrieved his pocket Game Boy from his nightstand. Sliding in a cartridge of "Tetris," he switched the game on and curled up in bed, this time keeping the game's volume, which usually blasted a traditional Russian folk song, all the way down so not even his mom's supersensitive ears could detect it. As he maneuvered the game's spinach-colored puzzle blocks into position, he was interrupted once more. This time, the disturbance came from his desk drawer across the room.

"Rinnie! Rinnie, are you there?" It was Robert, calling from his walkie-talkie. Instinctively, Rinnie switched his game off and rushed over to the drawer to answer the call before it alerted his mother again.

"Robert?" he asked into the speaker part of the device. "What are you doing up so early? And how are you able to reach me? You must be in close range."

"I am," Robert said. "Look outside your window."

Rinnie lifted his window shade and saw Robert on his walkie-talkie sitting on his bike in the driveway. Rinnie panicked. "Rob," he began, shutting the shade once more. "What are you doing? My dad's going to be leaving for work soon, and if he catches you—"

"He's not," Robert interrupted. "Not if you come outside now."

"What?" Rinnie asked, dumbfounded. "You've gotta be crazy! It's six in the morning. Why would I do that?"

Though Rinnie couldn't see it, Robert gave an easy smile. "Because I'm going to climb Danger Peak."

Rinnie blinked rapidly as if a flashlight had been shone in his eyes. Based on the resolve in Robert's voice, he knew his friend wasn't joking and that he couldn't change his mind.

"I'm coming down now," he said.

"Great," Robert replied. "I know your bike's still in the shop, so you can ride with me. And don't forget your walkie-talkie."

"Got it," Rinnie said. "Over and out."

With that, he switched off his device and headed for his bedroom door. Passing by his wall-length mirror in the shape of a giant Swatch watch, he caught a glimpse of himself and swallowed hard. "I can't believe we're actually going to do this."

◡

Similar to Robert, Chris had been tossing and turning all night. It was unusually warm that October evening, and his bedsheets were soaked with sweat. He thought he may have been coming down with a fever, but he knew it was what was on his mind that was truly burning him up. Scaling Danger Peak had been Robert's obsession all along, and Chris had even teased him about it, but over the past week, through their many trials and misadventures, it had become something of a fascination for him as well. Every time their club made an advancement to their bike, there was another setback, and it seemed, with all the trouble from their teachers, parents, and even the cops, when it came to completing their dream, it was either now or never.

To set his mind at ease, Chris grabbed a remote and turned on his small rabbit-eared television set in the corner of his room, but the images that first flickered on the screen were far from comforting. An early-morning rerun of a hard-hitting magazine news show was highlighting protests outside the Berlin Wall. People on the east side of the concrete barrier were trying to join friends and loved ones on the other side of the divide, but armed guards blocked their attempted reunion. In the back of his mind, almost subconsciously, Chris thought about his club's own struggles.

Chris flipped on MTV. Billy Joel was singing behind a table that had been set on fire. He then switched the TV off when his walkie-talkie lit up on his nightstand like a ghost in the machine.

"Hello, Chris?" a voice asked. "Are you up?" Chris didn't need to ask who it was or even what he wanted. He'd been best friends with Robert since kindergarten, and at this point, they were almost psychically linked. He grabbed the communicator without thinking.

"Let's do this," he said.

24

SAYING GOODBYE

The Wild Boars stared at the rusty gate sign only inches away: "DANGER PEAK." Just beyond the sign was the mountainous landmark itself. There was no going back now. With Rinnie sitting behind him, Robert slowly rode his dirt bike past the gate opening, with Chris, as ever, following close behind on his bike. When they reached the mountain base, they each switched off their motors and dismounted to say their goodbyes. No one wanted to admit the obvious jeopardy involved in scaling the mountain. Hell, the word "Danger" was in its very name. Instead, they attempted small talk about the weather as a cool wind rustled a few cranberry- and canary-flecked leaves past their sneakers.

"Why aren't you wearing a jacket?" Chris asked. "You must be freezing."

"I didn't want to risk getting caught by my parents," Robert explained, visibly shivering in the wind. "I was just grounded for a month."

"I know the feeling," Chris sympathized.

"Here, take mine," Rinnie offered, removing his coat to hand it to Robert. "You need it more than me."

"Thanks, Rinnie," he said, momentarily placing the coat on his bike seat. "I've got something for you too."

"You do?" Rinnie asked, more than a little surprised.

"Yeah," he replied. "Check my secret compartment." Rinnie did so and discovered his oversized, floppy novelty hat, with the mini laser still stashed inside. Robert removed the laser and handed Rinnie his hat.

"My hat!" he cheered like a five-year-old while happily putting it on.

Chris shook his head yet still smiled affectionately. "Try not to lose it before Halloween," he said.

Robert began tying the laser onto his handlebar with some steel wire he had taken from his father's toolbox. "Listen, Rinnie," he began, "I know we put you through a lot, but you've always come through for us in the end."

"Yeah," Chris agreed, clapping Rinnie on the back.

"Thanks, guys," Rinnie enthused, almost flushing red as he wasn't used to all the compliments.

Then Robert put on Rinnie's coat, and he was swimming in it. "Geez, Rin," he said, "you really need to try

SlimFast." Chris immediately broke into that familiar, high-pitched cackle of his that Robert had grown to love over the years.

"Hey!" Rinnie shouted. Now his face was red for a different reason.

"We're just kidding, man," Robert said.

"Yeah," Chris agreed. "You have a great sense of humor, so you should be able to take a joke."

Rinnie stared blankly at the air and then weakly replied, "Thanks . . . I think."

"Oh no!" Robert suddenly snapped. Both Chris and Rinnie whipped their faces toward him.

"What's the problem, man?" Chris asked.

"In all the commotion, I forgot to refuel!" Robert explained. The trio gazed at Robert's gas gauge, and sure enough, the indicator was sloping toward empty. "I'll never make it up there now."

Chris thought a moment and then had a brainstorm. "Here!" he shouted and raced around to the back compartment of his motorbike. "You can siphon the gas out of my tank. I just filled up myself by siphoning the gas out of my old man's car this afternoon," he explained as he produced a clear rubber tube about six feet long.

"Thanks, Chris," Robert began, "but how are you guys going to get back?"

"Don't worry," Chris answered as he opened his gas tank and placed the rubber hose in. "It's not that far. We'll walk it back."

"What's all this 'we' stuff?" Rinnie asked, slightly

annoyed. The guys ignored him as Robert opened his gas tank and Chris began sucking from one end of the hose. In a matter of seconds, the gasoline from Chris's tank begin funneling through his tube. It then spewed forth at the end and almost completely doused his face before he violently jerked it back, gagging on the fumes.

"Quick," Robert panicked. "Put the other end in my tank!" Chris did so and gave him a look as if to say, "What did you *think* I was going to do? Plug up my butt?" It was a rare moment of sarcasm aimed at his leader.

As Chris methodically siphoned the gas from his tank to Robert's, there was a nervous tension in the air. Chris felt like they were preparing for a space shuttle launch. Still, he was proud he was contributing something to the mission.

"That should do it," Robert said as the indicator for his fuel tank pointed to full. "Thanks."

"No problem," Chris said as he removed the tube from Robert's tank and screwed the cap back on. He then placed the tube back into his bike's rear compartment and tightened the lid on his own gas tank.

Robert craned his head to look toward the summit of Danger Peak. This was it. There was no turning back now. It was uncomfortably quiet, almost as if he were having second thoughts, when Chris broke the silence by pointing at Robert's left foot and asking, "How's your ankle?"

Robert smirked. "It's as good as it's ever going to

be," he said. "Besides, my mom wrapped it last night, and there's no more time anyway." He then turned his attention to the ominous mountaintop of Danger Peak, and his friends' gazes followed. The summit was shielded by a gathering thick fog, and even if the weather were clear, they still couldn't have seen the top from ground level.

"I have to admit part of me is jealous," Chris divulged, "but the other part just thinks you're nuts."

"I'm not nuts," Robert said, slamming the visor on his helmet down with a definitive swipe. "I'm a Wild Boar."

Chris grinned. "Just have fun?" he asked, outstretching his hand, palm down.

"Just have fun," Robert and Rinnie repeated their club's motto and placed their hands on top of Chris's. Robert flipped on the laser mounted to his handlebar like he was firing up a Ghostbuster proton pack, ready for action. He then switched on his bike's engine and revved it a few times for dramatic emphasis.

"Don't forget to keep your walkie-talkies on," he instructed his club members.

"Will do," Chris immediately responded.

"Sure thing," Rinnie agreed. Then, just before Robert turned his sights toward his destiny, Rinnie added, "Good luck!"

Robert smiled confidently. "I don't need luck," he said, patting the side of his beloved bike. "I've got the Action Bike."

And with that, Robert was off, driving away to

leave his fellow club members behind in a swarm of dust. Chris wanted to ride alongside him, but he was practical enough to realize only one of their bikes had a ghost of a chance to climb Danger Peak, and it sure wasn't his. Rinnie, for his part, not only still had his bike in the shop, but even if it were fixed, he'd be too cowardly to attempt the climb. While the other two Wild Boars wouldn't physically be on that mountain with their leader, they would be in spirit.

25

UP DANGER PEAK

Robert quickly found the dirt path that lined the edge of the mountain, and he wondered just how far it would wind upward before disappearing. Just to make sure it was working, he flipped on his walkie-talkie to the correct frequency and announced, "Okay, guys, I found the trail." Afterward, there was silence on the other end, and he stared at his device in unbearable suspense, making sure to also keep his attention on the rough mountainous terrain in front of him. *Have they been caught by their parents?* he thought. *Or, worse, the cops?*

Turning around to peer behind him as his bike climbed ever higher, he could still see their tiny shadows at the mountain base, and he breathed a sigh of relief. But upon turning his head forward again, he saw a sharp curve in the trail only several feet away, and he swerved his bike sideways to narrowly miss it. His dad's tires violently jerked beneath him as he noticed the trail was getting bumpier. Finally, his walkie-talkie came alive with the sound of his friends.

"Alright, Robert," Chris said. "Looking good so far. Keep going!"

"Yeah," Rinnie added, "we can still see you!"

Feeling their support flow through his movements, Robert revved the motor into high gear. "Okay," he said. "This is for us." After stashing his communicator into his secret compartment, he popped a wheelie and screamed forward. He felt like he could take on the world. With his friends by his side, there was nothing he couldn't do.

As Robert's town became smaller and smaller while he climbed higher and higher, he began to realize that all the problems of the townsfolk below, including his own, didn't seem as significant anymore—at least not as much as when he was on ground level. From God's vantage point, he reasoned, everything seemed less important, yet because of life's fragility, somehow everything seemed much more precious.

Ironically, Robert had always been afraid of heights, so as he and his bike climbed ever upward, he made sure not to look down too often. He was almost dizzy from the advanced elevation, and the thin air was making it harder to breathe. On top of that, the beautifully clear morning had suddenly given way to a thick fog. Like a grumpy giant in some children's fairy tale, it was as if Danger Peak itself didn't wish to be disturbed. As the fog gathered, it made it increasingly difficult to see, and Robert was fighting a headache from his sprained ankle, which was still sore. Up and around the mountain, he followed the path until it became impenetrable. Eventually, the trail completely disappeared beneath him, and he was riding blind.

After several more minutes of carefully maneuvering his bike up the side of the mountain, in the back of his mind, Robert wondered if his friends could still see him. Though he could guess the answer, a fearful side of him didn't want to know. Still, his greater, braver side was curious, and that part is what ultimately prevailed. With one hand still steadily steering his dream machine, Robert carefully reached behind him to open the secret compartment. After flipping open the latch, he reached even farther to grab his walkie-talkie.

Excitedly tuning the dial into his friends' agreed-upon frequency, he called out, "Guys, are you there? It's me, Robert." He would've slapped his forehead in embarrassment if he didn't need to keep his balance on the rugged terrain. *Who else would it be?* he asked himself. *The Stay Puft Marshmallow Man?*

There was no response, so Robert tried again. "Chris?" he called out to the void. "Rinnie? *Anybody?*"

Silence. It was then that Robert truly felt alone. Lost in thought and not paying attention, he rode over a hollowed-out crater, and the bounce of the bike threw his walkie-talkie to the ground, instantly shattering it to pieces—and with it, his final contact to the world below.

To add insult to injury, the fog misting the pathway now enveloped him into a thick shroud. Robert flipped on his high beams, but similar to a car's headlights, they only shone distractingly back at him, forming a glare in his visor, so he turned them back off. Before he could complain about the fog, as if in a twisted game of one-upmanship, the weather worsened. Storm clouds began gathering overhead, and Robert realized he must be getting closer to the top. He sighed with relief, until a dramatic flash of lightning erupted in the sky, seemingly inches from his face. The skin of his arms practically sizzled from the heat, and he felt like he was entering a boxing ring with Zeus himself.

Another electric strike tore a hole in the path directly in front of him, sending a mound of dirt flying into his face, and Robert had to quickly weave around it to avoid falling in. After narrowly missing that pitfall, yet another bolt ripped through the atmosphere and shook his tiny bike asunder, the flash almost blinding him. He felt the next one might not miss its mark. It's as if someone—or something—didn't want him to reach the top.

"Hold together, baby," he told his bike. Still another lightning bolt lit up the sky. The one positive aspect of the sudden change in weather was that for brief moments during each flash, Robert could see everything in his path.

That's when the rain came pouring down in sheets.

It formed tiny rivulets in the makeshift road, the shifting sands and rocks beneath his bike making it progressively difficult to navigate his way to the top. The water pelted his visor hard, and he wished he had a miniature window wiper to clear it off. The idea sounded like something Dr. Howard would invent, and Robert fleetingly considered the irony of how his ex-technology teacher had inadvertently helped him achieve his goal.

Yet more thunder rang in his ears. Well, *almost* achieve his goal. He wasn't out of the woods—or, more accurately, mountain—yet. Robert realized that all he needed to get through this sudden storm was a boost in speed. That's when he felt like a fool. After all, it's not like he was riding an average, everyday dirt bike. He had built the Action Bike for this very purpose.

Blindly feeling the wet metallic body lashed with rain, with one hand he finally located what he was seeking and firmly pushed the miniature button of the turbocharger. Instantaneously, the vehicle rocketed to a cool sixty miles per hour, quickly bypassing the fog and rain. He was moving so fast, in fact, it looked like someone had sucked up the fog in a giant vacuum cleaner.

Because he had never attempted a boost on a vertical slope, Robert could feel himself losing control of his bike, and the turbocharger wheezed with a great whine. Before he could switch it off, there was a sharp bang from the enhanced attachment, and it belched a dark cloud of smoke, its power fizzling away to nothing.

Robert realized the turbocharger broke, but it mattered little; it had accomplished the job he had set out for it to do. He stroked his brother's invention like he was petting a spaniel before putting it to sleep.

"Sorry, Danny," he apologized.

Looking ahead, it seemed that he was in the clear. There was no more rain, thunder, or even fog to contend with. Robert smiled brightly and thought of one of his favorite lines from *Ghostbusters*: "Well, that wasn't such a chore now, was it?"

That's when a giant boulder came smashing down in front of him, almost destroying the Action Bike in the process. *How could I be so stupid?* Robert asked himself, echoing his father. *How could I forget the boulders?*

Giving himself some grace, Robert realized that so much had happened up to that point that it was easy to get distracted from the real danger of Danger Peak: the impromptu landslide. The one that no one had yet survived. Another, smaller boulder flew by his safety helmet. Then another, this time larger than the first. Yet another raced by, almost glancing his side. They kept coming, like a hailstorm in the land of giants, and Robert wondered exactly where their origin was. They seemingly came out of nowhere, like some secret portal, and Robert weaved his bike in and out of the falling boulders while thinking of Han Solo deftly navigating the Millennium Falcon through an asteroid field.

Before he could contemplate just where the large rocks were coming from, this time, Robert no longer hesitated. Charging up his miniature laser cannon, he did what it had been brought there for: obliterating boulders to smithereens. As he repeatedly fired the laser, red bolts split the boulders into pieces. Large boulders fragmented into smaller ones, and smaller ones disintegrated into dust. Dark sand exploded into Robert's visor, and he wiped it off with the back of his arm. For a moment, the boulders stopped coming.

Robert rode up into the clouds themselves as if he were entering the gates of heaven. As the clouds parted, he could at last glimpse the top of Danger Peak, and it was magnificent. He triumphantly cheered, pumping one fist in the air, when he was suddenly hit with another massive boulder.

At that point, he only saw black.

26

AN UNEXPECTED ENCOUNTER

"Robert?" an older, loving voice called. "Robert, wake up."

Robert blinked his eyes open and found himself surrounded by pinkish-white cotton balls of clouds. He was lying down on very rocky ground, and in the corner of one eye, he glanced his bike on its side several feet away, still in one piece but visibly the worse for wear.

Robert sat up, removed his helmet, and looked around. The huge, warm sun was so close that he thought he could touch it, but its heat and light weren't overpowering. It just felt welcoming. Even though the immediate area was clear and beautiful, he could still spot lightning crackling in the far distance, signaling the storm had passed. In short, the view was absolutely breathtaking. Since he was near the edge, he peered over to spot the tiny outline of his town below as if he were viewing it from the window of a 747. He had made it. He had scaled Danger Peak.

Robert tried standing, but a strong arm steadied him from behind. "Easy there."

Turning around, Robert recognized someone he had thought he'd never see again.

"Danny?" he asked, not believing his eyes. It was really him. Filled with youthful energy, and handsome as ever, Danny didn't look a day older than the last time Robert had seen him. In fact, he was wearing the exact same outfit as that day in his bedroom: ripped blue jeans and a stylish black T-shirt.

"Have you been up here all this time?"

"Yep," he replied. "Looking down on all you guys."

Robert rushed to embrace his older brother, the pinkish clouds dancing as he hurried past.

"But," Robert began, backing away, "how have you stayed alive all this time? You've been gone over a year."

Danny didn't respond; he only looked at his little brother with pity in his big brown eyes as if he didn't understand what he was saying. With no answer, Robert repeated himself: "What are you doing here?"

Danny smiled that famously confident grin of his that Robert often tried to imitate. "I wanted to tell you how proud I am of you, Robert," he began. "It's amazing how much you've grown up. I can't believe it's only been a year."

"Well, thirteen is a lot different from twelve," Robert said with remarkable self-awareness.

"You're right," Danny agreed. "And I've watched you deal with Dad the best way you could. I know how aggressive he can be."

"That's an understatement," Robert said.

"Maybe," Danny admitted, "but also realize Dad is doing the best that *he* can. He wasn't raised by loving parents like we were."

Robert was taken aback. "Dad is *loving*?" he asked.

"I know it doesn't seem that way, but he does care about you, Robert," Danny solemnly said. "He worries about you. He just has a funny way of showing it."

"That's what Mom said," Robert replied.

"You know that Mom loves you with all of her heart," Danny added.

Robert nodded. "I know."

"Take care of her. You're her only son now."

"Okay," Robert said, looking at the bandage still on his wounded ankle.

Danny then knitted his eyebrows as if to signal a shift in tone. It was clear his message wasn't going to be all sunshine and rainbows. "Robert," he began more seriously, "I *do* have to warn you too."

"About what?" Robert asked in trepidation.

"I've noticed you getting in trouble with the police," he said sternly, "and I don't like it. You shouldn't steal. It's wrong."

Robert's pulse quickened. The last thing he wanted to do was upset Danny, especially in whatever limbo world they were conversing. At the same time, he still stood his ground.

"I only stole what was rightfully yours!" he petulantly cried. "You invented the turbocharger. Dr. Howard stole it from you. I only stole it back!"

"Two wrongs don't make a right," Danny reasoned.

"Man," Robert began, "you mean that cliché is really true?"

"I'm not joking," Danny said, "and besides, you also stole Dr. Howard's laser. I didn't invent that."

Robert opened his mouth, prepared to continue the argument, but ultimately fought the impulse. He wondered how often he would have a chance to talk to his big brother. He didn't know how much time they had left, and he didn't want to waste it fighting.

"Okay," Robert conceded. "I'll give the laser back."

"And?" Danny asked expectantly.

Robert had to scan his brain to take his brother's hint, but when his eyes landed on his fallen bike, he finally understood. "Oh," he said, "and Dad's tires."

"Good," Danny said, smiling again.

Once more, Robert took in the atmosphere around them. They seemed to be halfway to heaven and yet still stuck on earth. He could feel the harsh ground beneath his sneakers, but his upper body felt like it was floating in space. After an awkward beat, Robert decided to ask, "What's it like, Danny?"

"What's what like?"

Robert paused. Then, summoning up the courage, "What's it like in heaven?"

Teasingly, Danny waited a few moments before responding, purposefully keeping him in suspense. It was one of his typical big-brother power moves, and Robert had to chuckle to himself in recognition of his game. Even after all this time, he was still the same ol' Danny, and their relationship felt as if no time had passed, like they had just seen each other the other day at home, with the older brother ribbing Robert to finish his homework early so they could work on his bike.

"It's hard to describe," Danny finally answered, "but it's wonderful." Robert smiled. "And it's only the beginning," Danny continued. "Our lives are long. Even after life. You'll see one day."

Robert suddenly didn't care that he had bested Danger Peak, and for a moment, it didn't even seem odd that he was talking to his brother. He was just happy to see him again, in whatever form. Daring himself, and with mist in his eyes, Robert asked, "Danny, do you wanna have a *Star Wars* sleepover? Maybe I can play Han this time."

Danny warmly smiled. "Not now, buddy," he replied. Then, as if something—or someone—was calling him, he added, "I have to go. I'll see you later. I promise."

Danny waved and began walking away, and Robert wondered where he could possibly be going since they were on top of a mountain. He tried to follow but found he was stuck to the earth, like in a bad dream. He couldn't move, no matter how hard he struggled.

"No, wait!" he called out to his departing brother. "Danny!" It was bad enough that Danny had to leave Robert's life once already, but now he was stranding him again. "Don't leave, Danny!" Robert desperately cried. "Don't leave me alone!"

As Danny disappeared completely into the mist, Robert heard his final words. "You're not alone."

27

WHERE AM I?

"Robert?" someone called, shaking him from slumber. "Robert, wake up." It was the identical greeting Robert had heard at the top of Danger Peak, only its voice was softer. Robert stirred awake and looked around.

"Danny?" he asked the voice. Even though his eyes were open, he still couldn't make out the figures in front of him. They resembled gray blobs.

"He thinks his brother's still alive," a deeper voice explained.

"Who's that?" Robert asked. "Where am I?" Soon, his eyesight returned, and Robert found himself lying on a hospital bed. His parents were on either side, and he was suddenly reminded of the famous finale of *The Wizard of Oz*. He tried to get up, but an IV tugged at his arm. Robert squealed in pain.

"Shh," his mother hushed, gently placing her hand

on her son's chest. "Lie down, honey. You had us all worried sick. Thank God you're okay." Robert suddenly realized it was her voice that had awakened him.

His father looked his son's body over: his right leg was in a cast; his left ankle was still sprained; and in the rare areas where there wasn't a white bandage, purplish bruises on his skin were peeking out. "Well, *okay* is a relative term," he said a bit bluntly. Then, shaking his head, he added, "Robert, what in the world were you thinking? You almost died on that mountain like Danny."

"Where am I?" Robert asked again.

"You're at South Shore Hospital," an authoritative voice explained. Turning his head past his mother on the right, Robert realized there was someone else, a doctor, in the room. He was wearing a long white coat and carrying an official-looking clipboard. "You were discovered near the top of Danger Peak by helicopter," the doctor continued. Robert was instantly uncomfortable. He hated hospitals. He considered them a place where people go to die. As if he were reading his mind, the doctor said, "Frankly, it's a miracle we were able to save you, considering what happened to your brother."

"But he's alive," Robert protested. "I saw him."

"What?" his mother asked, clutching her chest and looking as if she had just seen a ghost.

"Danny," Robert repeated, somewhat unnecessarily. "I was with him, like only an hour ago."

The doctor clucked his tongue in sympathy. "Robert," he began, "I'm afraid you suffered a concussion and sustained multiple internal injuries. We felt it necessary to put you in a medically induced coma."

Robert lurched in surprise at the news, once again tugging his IV drip and smarting his arm. "No," Robert said, "that's not possible. I was just talking to Danny."

Now Robert's father was getting impatient. "Robert," he started, "your bike was smashed by a boulder. You were found near the top of Danger Peak."

"Right," Robert said, "that's where I found Danny."

His father threw his hands in the air. "He's delusional," he informed the doctor.

"I'll give you guys some time to talk," the doctor politely said before excusing himself from the room.

Desperately wanting to believe her son, his mother asked, "What did he look like, Robert?"

Robert thought for a moment, screwing his eyes to the back of his head as if they were the ones retrieving the memory. "He looked the same," he answered. "He looked great." His mother's smile spread across her face like a blooming rose. It was clear it was what she wanted—even needed—to hear.

Suddenly, a thought occurred to him. "How did you know where I was?"

"Your friends told us," his mom explained. "Apparently, they felt guilty for letting you perform such a dangerous stunt and came to get us after you didn't come back."

"Yeah," his father chimed in, "and it's a good thing they did, or we wouldn't have gotten the chopper there in time. Then we wouldn't be standing around your hospital bed. We'd be standing around your casket." Donna gave Stan a disapproving glare as if he crossed some unspoken boundary.

"Where are they?" Robert asked. "Where's Chris and Rinnie?"

"They're right outside, honey," his mom explained. "The doctor noticed you stirring this morning and realized you might wake soon, so we called them to come over."

"Can I see them?"

"Of course," she said, turning toward the door to retrieve them.

Stan was less sympathetic. "Make it quick," he said and joined his wife to the side.

Donna opened the door to usher in his friends. "Boys," she called, "you can come on in. He's up!"

Chris and Rinnie excitedly hurried into the room like little kids stomping down the stairs in their Underoos on Christmas morning. Robert felt like he hadn't seen them in ages. Too much had happened since the last time they saw each other.

"You did it, man!" Chris said, going in for a high five but then thinking better of it after eyeing the IV drip.

"Yeah!" Rinnie cheered, brushing past Robert's parents to stand near the other side of the bed.

"Well, *almost*," Robert admitted. "They said I was found near the top."

"Still," Chris said, "we're just glad you're alive."

Rinnie nodded, a rare moment of solidarity between them.

"How are things at school?" Robert asked.

"Rinnie has a date," Chris announced.

Robert did a comical double-take like Max Headroom. "What?" he asked, as if that were the most shocking thing that had happened to him that week. "With who?"

"Barbara," Rinnie said with pride.

Now Robert's neck almost snapped in two from the whiplash. "Am I still hallucinating?"

"I know," Chris said, sheepishly surveying the floor. "I can't believe it either."

"How is this possible?" Robert asked.

"I ran into her at the Halloween dance," Rinnie began explaining.

Just then, Robert realized he'd been in the hospital long enough to miss his favorite holiday. "I missed Halloween?" he asked like a petulant child.

"You missed a lot of things, buddy," Chris answered, practically rubbing it in. "The Berlin Wall is even coming down." Robert whistled in disbelief as Rinnie appeared aggravated at having his story interrupted.

"*Anyway*," Rinnie continued, visibly annoyed, "we were at the Halloween dance at school, and she loved my costume. I guess she has a thing for floppy hats."

The three laughed with full hearts. "For your sake, Rin," Chris added, pointing to Rinnie's pants, "I hope she also has a thing for floppy d—" He then caught a glimpse of Stan's stern face. "Uh, *disks*," he ad-libbed to save face. "Yeah, floppy disks because you love playing those videogames of yours so much."

Stan looked on with disapproving eyes, and Robert's smile wilted into a frown. "I guess you guys have to go," he said. "Thanks for checking in on me."

"Anytime," Rinnie said.

"I wish I was up there with you, man," Chris said with a wistful gleam in his green eyes.

"Yeah, me too," Rinnie added.

Robert paused a moment and then smiled. "You guys were," he said. Chris and Rinnie smiled back and then turned to leave, but Robert stopped them by reaching out weakly with one hand. "Hey," he said, "we had fun, didn't we, guys?"

After briefly mulling over their various misadventures together, Chris and Rinnie grinned.

"Yeah," Chris agreed.

"Sure did," added Rinnie.

They then stacked their hands, palms down, on each other in their familiar club salute, and Chris and Rinnie left the room.

When the door closed behind them, and it was clear they were out of earshot, Stan turned to his son. "Robert," he began, "I shouldn't have bought you that blasted bike in the first place. But you saw how happy Danny was when he got his bike, and you desperately wanted your own." He waited for a response, and when it didn't come, he reluctantly continued talking. "We should've taken your bike away as soon as Danny died on Danger Peak."

Robert winced at his words, as if having his bike taken from him would've been a fate worse than actually dying on the mountain. "Anyway, that would've been the easier thing to do. It's not like we could've moved the mountain," he added with a wry grin.

"Where *is* my bike?" Robert asked.

"It's back in our shed," his father explained. "Well, what's left of it. The laser was returned to Dr. Howard, but since Danny invented the turbocharger, he agreed to let us keep it."

"He did?" Robert asked, beside himself.

"Yeah," his father said. "He realized how much it must've meant to you for you to take it from his closet like that." It seemed Robert's teacher had a heart after all.

Robert scrolled through the mental checklist of the parts he'd used to improve his dirt bike. "I guess you also figured out I took your tires," he said sheepishly.

"Yeah, it was fairly obvious, Robert," his father replied. Robert bowed his head in shame, as low as he could make it in a hospital bed. "Remarkably, the tires weren't damaged on the mountain, so I've already put them back on my car."

"I'm sorry I took them, Dad. I guess I was just mad at you and wanted to get a little revenge."

"Two wrongs don't make a right." Danny's words

came out of his father's mouth, and Robert momentarily wondered if that's where Danny had gotten the expression in the first place. "Robert," Stan continued, softening his normally stiff posture, "I know I've been hard on you lately, and maybe I even drove you to do something this dangerous. I can't help feeling like I'm partly to blame."

Stan gazed dolefully at his son's broken body, waiting patiently for a response, and Robert thought of something Danny had told him. "You're doing the best you can," he told his Dad.

"I am," he admitted, "and I know now that sometimes that isn't enough." He then stared at the floor, afraid to utter the next part. "You must know I haven't been the same since Danny left us. You've had some huge shoes to fill, and I suppose it wasn't fair of me to put that burden on you."

Robert smirked half-heartedly. He knew it was as close to an apology as his father was going to give. And he decided to take it.

"Okay, Dad," he said.

Unexpectedly, Robert's father began choking back a few tears. "Okay," he said, cracking a tear-stained smile.

Donna was beaming proudly as Robert turned toward her. "Mom," he began, "I wanted you to know something too."

"What's that, sweetie?" she asked, almost crying herself.

"I'll always be there for you," he said.

Now Donna *was* crying. "That's all I've ever wanted," she gushed, moving in for a hug.

"Alright, alright," Stan said, attempting to cut the treacle. "Let's hold ourselves together here." But Robert and his mom ignored him and continued their embrace. Eventually, Stan surrendered and joined them.

As the three family members hugged on Robert's bed—with his parents careful not to disturb that pesky IV drip—Robert contemplated the eventful past week. He thought of what he'd originally set out to do—climbing Danger Peak—and realized he had accomplished so much more. He'd proven his worth to his friends, his parents, and his town—but more importantly, to himself. And he learned the ultimate lesson: dreams do come true.

EPILOGUE

Two months later

Still walking with a limp, Robert cautiously approached the familiar chain-link fence he had grown to simultaneously love and fear, but there was nothing familiar about what lay beyond it. He had heard the reports, but he still couldn't believe his eyes. Danger Peak was gone. Sometime in the middle of the night, it had sunk straight into the ground and was swallowed by the earth, leaving a giant crater that could fit the Empire State Building. If someone had wanted to try to match Robert's achievement of climbing the mountain and reaching the top now, that time had clearly passed.

It wasn't just what he had accomplished, but his new battle scars—the evidence of that momentous climb—scored him popularity points at school. He noticed a few attractive girls looking at him a little longer than they had before, and most of the jocks in the hallway parted to give him room. He suspected he had even earned the respect of Vinny, though, of course, the bully would never admit it. At least he had stopped spray-painting Rinnie's locker.

Robert wondered what it all meant. Was Danger Peak a test just for him? Did he really see Danny at the top that fateful day, or was it simply a delusion as his father and doctor had insisted? Was Danger Peak actually a gateway to the Other Side?

Robert figured he'd probably never know, and maybe it was just as well. It was a new month in a new year of a new decade. Anything could happen.

THE END

ACKNOWLEDGMENTS

Special thanks to the following:

God, without whom nothing is possible.

My lovely wife Camille, for putting up with me. I know it hasn't been easy.

My beautiful daughters Samantha and Marisa, for making life worthwhile.

My sister Patricia, for being my first reader.

My Mom, for being my first teacher and providing moral support.

My Dad, for being my first critic and providing financial support.

My beta readers Vince, Linnet, and Damian, for their invaluable feedback.

My Sixth Grade teacher Mr. Joyce, for telling me I was the "finest creative writer" he ever taught.

Made in United States
North Haven, CT
27 June 2022

20661823R00117